LIVING LA VIDA MOCHA

**COFFEE LOFT
SERIES**

H.M. SHANDER

Living La Vida Mocha
Published by H.M. Shander
Copyright 2024 H.M. Shander

ISBN (paperback) 978-1-990240-25-6
ISBN (e-book) 978-1-990240-23-2

Living La Vida Mocha is a work of fiction. Names,
characters, places and incidents either are the
products of the author's imagination or are used
factitiously. Any resemblances to actual persons,
living or dead, events or locals, are entirely
coincidental.

Cover Design: Rebecca from Beck and Dot
Editing by: PWA & IDIM Editorial
Shander, H.M., 1975—Living La Vida Mocha
First Edition

Titles by H.M. Shander

Duly Noted – book 1
That Summer – book 2
If You Say Yes – book 3
Serving Up Innocence
Serving Up Devotion
Serving Up Secrecy
Serving Up Hope
It All Began with a Note
It All Began with a Mai-Tai
It All Began with a Wedding
Noel
Whistler's Night
Dreamers in Cheshire Bay
Return to Cheshire Bay
Adrift in Cheshire Bay
Awake in Cheshire Bay
Christmas in Cheshire Bay
Journey to Cheshire Bay
Charmed in Cheshire Bay
Second Chances in Cheshire Bay
Unforgiven in Cheshire Bay
Flirty in Cheshire Bay
Messages & Mistletoe
Living La Vida Mocha

Chapter One

MY TESLA ROLLED silently to a stop at the red light, and I wished the moments in my life stopped with as much grace.

The screen on the display flashed with an incoming call; my boss, Tory. Hitting the answer button, I allowed his voice to boom through the in-car speakers.

"Hey, Tory."

"Listen, Cara, I don't have long. Are you out and about?" He never had *long* for anything. Not for meetings, tolerance, or phone calls.

"Yeah. I'm just running around. Getting ideas for the Mitchelson files."

A mother pushing a carriage meandered across the street, despite the 'don't walk' sign blinking

1

rapidly. This town drove me crazy with the incessant number of lights; no wonder it took forever to get from one side to the other.

"About that." There was a slight hesitation, or at least I thought there was. "Cara, I hate to do this while you're driving. Are you driving?"

A flurry of wicked butterflies took flight in my gut. Whatever he was about to say, it was sending out a flood of nervousness. "I'm parked at a light but yes, I'm driving."

"Doggone it." Muffled sounds in the background floated through the speakers.

A horn honked behind me, and I glared into the rear-view mirror as my foot pressed down on the accelerator.

"I hate to do this to you, but Cara, you're fired." There were no inflections, no pauses, no sighs – nothing indicated he had trouble voicing any of it.

The words came straight out of left field and sucker-punched me in the gut.

"I'm what?" Breathless, my foot came off the gas pedal to a flood of honking horns. My heart thundered against my ribs, threatening to escape as panic surged through me.

"Your office has been rekeyed. Your passwords will no longer work and as we speak, your personal items are being boxed up by Annabelle." My trusted personal assistant.

"Why?"

More horns blared, and I cranked the wheel to the right and took the first available turn. It happened to be a shopping mall parking lot devoid of many vehicles.

"You want to know?"

"I think I deserve to know."

Finally, a sigh ebbed out of him. "Fair enough. Frankly, you weren't our first pick for the Derry files, but with Michelle's abrupt medical leave, our hands were tied, and we had no one else who could cover. You make impulsive decisions, you're not listening to the client's needs, and you keep acting like a PR manager instead of the marketing rep they hired. You're just not a team player, Cara, and by this point in your career with Baker-Bloom, we expected more from you."

I slipped the car into the parking stall and put the vehicle into park, huffing out words that sounded like desperate gasps of air.

"Cara, are you still there?"

"Um, yeah, Tory, amazingly enough, I am still here." Physically maybe, but my head was swimming in an ocean of confusion.

"Annabelle will have your personal effects shipped out to you before the end of the day, and your final paycheck will be forthcoming."

"That's it? No warnings?"

"You've had several, and they've all been documented."

"Yeah, but those were minor." Absolutely nothing worth being fired over.

"You just refuse to make the changes. I'm sorry to do this to you in the middle of the day and wish it had happened in person, but you weren't here when I came into the office."

"Because I'm out looking for what Grant Mitchelson wanted and needed. I'm gathering ideas." *Like you suggested I do.* But I wasn't going to throw it back at him. When Tory made up his mind, that was the end of it.

"Jacob will take over for him effective immediately."

"Of course, he will." Mr. Brownnose the Second. He had his head so far up Tory's rear end I wasn't sure where Tory ended and Jacob began. He was probably the reason I just lost my job.

The line went dead. There wasn't a *goodbye* or a *good luck* or a *let's do coffee* later like I'd received in my other firings, just empty air. Figured. The call ended abruptly, and I tipped my head back against the headrest, staring out through the tinted glass roof of my car up to the impending snow-filled clouds.

There were only two people I could call right now to talk to or at least hear a voice of comfort. One was my best friend Amanda, but I knew from our morning text she was in court this afternoon so that call was out. The other was my boyfriend, Gerry, and desperately I tried to remember what was on his docket for the day. When nothing came to mind, I asked the car to dial his number.

"Hey." It was an unusual way to answer, but I let it slide.

"Hey, Ger. I'm having a moment."

"Oh yeah? Me too." There was a shuffling noise on his side of the line. "Just a second, guys. It's been a weird Wednesday."

"We could hashtag it." Yes, it was desperate to grab for a lifeline of dumb funniness as I was already grasping, but I didn't know what else to do.

I sunk deeper and tapped the heater button to warm the seat. A deep, bone-chilling sense of cold had wrapped around my body and without warning, I shuddered violently.

On his end of the line, something crashed.

"Hey, guys, be gentle."

"Gerry? What's going on?"

"Awe, jeez, I'm not going to be of much help. Give me a minute. Not you, Car, the guys."

"Oh, okay." A solid lump of throat-choking pain dropped into the pit of my stomach. My words were breathless and void of any of the emotions swirling inside my head.

"Oh man, Cara, I hate to do this over the phone."

Oh no! Please, no.

"This isn't working out with us, and…" A long, earth-shattering exhale. "I'm breaking up with you."

"What?" Tentacles of lancing pain wrapped around my heart and constricted. Not only was I struggling to breathe, but I was also fighting to hold onto any form of consciousness. It all had to be a dream. I pinched myself and yelped. Nope, not a dream.

"Cara, I can't stand the way you eat your breakfast cereal." It came out in a whoosh.

I shook my head. "What? You're breaking up with me over the way I have my breakfast?"

"It's more than that, but jeez-Louise. That's just… It's wrong."

The staccato of my heart picked up in intensity.

"Although you eat cereal like a serial killer, it's more than that. Can you even tell me where I'm going this weekend?"

At that moment, I couldn't even tell him what my name was, how was I supposed to have remembered where he was? All I saw was a box of Mini Wheats, a bowl of milk, and a spoon. What was wrong with that?

"Cara?"

Right, that was my name. My breath was as frozen as the exterior air.

"Cara, can you hear me?"

I nodded. "I don't believe this." Cereal? That was the hill he was going to die on?

"Toronto, remember? I'm flying to Miami for Digger's wedding. The one you said you were too busy to attend. Because you had work to do. Always had the work."

It wasn't that I was too busy, it was more along the lines of I couldn't stand Digger and whatever his bride-to-be's name was, and while I wished them well, spending thousands of dollars to attend that freak show wasn't on my agenda. However, I had told Gerry he had my blessing to go, but I didn't remember the wedding being this weekend.

My knuckles turned white as I clenched the steering wheel trying to pull the heat from it into my cold hands. Cereal and a lack of remembering his weird friend's wedding – that was the catalyst for a breakup?

Gerry blew out his breath into the speaker. "I need more than just a bit of arm candy. I need someone who'll pay me a bit of attention, and not just when she needs a refill of her wine glass. I need someone I can talk to when that's what I need, not when you have a moment between files and clients. Cara, I needed you to be focused on me every once in a while, but you kept shoving me aside for work. I wasn't important to you. Not at all."

"That's not true." Because it wasn't. I did need him. That's why he was the one I was calling now.

"I moved a few of my things from your apartment back to mine last week. Did you even notice?"

Wracking my brain, I came up empty. Everything seemed to be the same, and nothing was misplaced or moved or randomly set someplace to be noticed. "Of course, I did."

"Tell me one thing that's missing."

Closing my eyes, I mentally swept my bedroom, the office, the bathroom, the living room, and all throughout the kitchen, trying to recall or visualize something out of place. Sadly, all I saw was the breakfast layout.

"You can't remember because it wasn't important enough to you because it wasn't work-related. I wasn't important to you for the very same reason." His voice hitched. Good grief, was he crying?

"Oh, Gerry." My tone tightened and a surge of anger flared. How could he do this to me? Today. Right now. Five minutes after being canned?

"Goodbye, Cara. Please don't call me again." With that, the call ended.

What in the world? Two phone calls in a matter of minutes, and I wasn't allowed to debate the issue, or give a defense statement? Amanda would lose her mind.

I smacked the steering wheel, screamed as loud as I could, and for as long as my breath held out, and fell like a weighted blanket back into the contours of my seat, staring out at the world around me.

The first snowflakes fell and melted on the windshield, turning into tiny pools of water.

What was I going to do with my life now?

After two years with Baker-Bloom, in a single

whoosh, I was jobless. Because why? Because I wasn't a team player? Did everyone have to be a team player like the brown-nosing Jacob? I worked better alone, because I understood what the expectations were, and I didn't have to wait for some slacker to get his or her butt in gear and get the job done. Doing the job right the first time was a quality I rose to exceed, and I expected it as much from my colleagues. Too often, they disappointed me, running home to be with their significant others or to play with their children, which was all fine and dandy, but maybe they should've worked smarter and harder while at the office.

Well, screw Tory and his team.

I faded into my memories of successful projects, and of the launch parties of our clients, although a waste of time. One could be back home or in the office working on another project. Maybe that's why Tory let me go. It wasn't the work; it was the partying after I hated. The dressing up, the mingling with clients, and putting on a brave smile when I felt smothered in the crowds and couldn't breathe. That was it. It had to be.

I shook my head and repositioned myself in the seat. Time to leave the parking lot, but before I left it in the dust, I spied a post office and threw a quick glance at the portfolio on the passenger seat. First, I needed to overnight all the paperwork and files to Tory, no sense holding onto those.

ONCE THE PACKAGE was sent, I sat back in my car as the snow fell in larger flakes. Putting the car in drive, I exited the parking lot and made a right turn, just driving. I had no rhyme or reason and put the retro playlist I'd discovered on Spotify. Sonic Youth came on first, and I cranked the volume until I couldn't hear the thoughts in my head.

As I drove out of town and hit the highway in excess of the speed limit, I let the music wrap around me and carry me away. It carried me quite the distance and after an hour of heading toward the towering mountains, I stumbled into another town, but this was far different than where I was from. This had old-world charm with quaint brick buildings from a hundred years ago, to rustic signs hanging above the storefronts. People scurried across the street, staring at me as I silently drove through.

I didn't drive into a big city; I drove into a Hallmark movie.

Finding an open parallel spot, I parked the car

and grabbed my fur-lined leather mitts and my Dior handbag. I zipped up my leather jacket and adjusted my silky scarf, gazing around at the flannel-crusted folk walking on the other side of the street.

Wherever I was, this was exactly what Grant Michelson was looking for. They canned me too soon because now I wasn't going to mention to anyone about this area; their loss. I hadn't looked on the map, and at the moment, didn't care. I wanted to see this town, this strip of movie magic, in the real.

Locking the car, I pocketed the keys and started meandering, pausing every once in a while under an overhanging to see and feel the strip in its full glory; with the snowflakes falling, the all-encompassing dampened silence, and the smell of freshness. The occasional car drove by, sloshing through the muddy pools of water, and I instinctively stepped further back lest I get sprayed.

I continued walking, taking it all in, full disbelief of what my senses were picking up. Surely this had to be a dream. The whole afternoon was. It had to be. If I blinked three times quick, I'd find I'd be back in my office lifting my head off the desk from a quick ten-minute snooze I needed because I'd been up until three a.m. working on a project.

One. Two. Three.

I opened my eyes, and everything was still the same. Doggone it. However, my gaze focused on a quaint shop – the Coffee Loft – and suddenly I was desperate for a steaming cup of something warm and comforting, plus a much-needed bathroom break. Looking both ways down the empty street, I crossed and made my way up the seven concrete steps leading into the brick building.

I had expected to hear bells ringing overhead as I opened the door, but there was no such thing. Not sure why I was so relieved, maybe it was the intoxicating aroma of freshly ground beans hanging in the air mixing with a healthy dose of cinnamon and baked bread zapping the waning disappointment. What was this place?

I shook my shoulders, dusted off the accumulated snow, and stomped my feet before walking over to the display case and drooling over the donuts. And all the pastries. And, oh my, they had trays of baked goods as well.

"Can I help you?" A young man asked.

"Just a minute, please." I threw a quick glance to the overhead board listing all the beverages. "They all sound amazing."

He simply nodded.

"I'll take one of these." I pointed to a thick, dark donut with white glaze, chocolate whipped cream decorated with shards and shavings of colourful candies. Gazing up at the menu board written in chalk, I scanned the drinks. "How about a Caramel Macchiato?"

He focused on the screen in front of him. "What size would you like?"

"What are my options?"

"We have tall, grande, venti, and lofty."

"Ooh, lofty sized? Sounds exactly like what I need." I laughed and slipped off my bag to rummage through for my phone. "I'll take one of those too please."

"In which mug?"

I wasn't sure I heard him correctly. "I'm sorry?"

"Pick your mug from the Mug Wall. Anything on the bottom shelf." With a bit of a dramatic flare, he pointed it out to me.

What I had thought was simply a huge painting, was, in fact, a recessed wall with a variety of mugs in every shape, size, and colour.

Spotting a *Mandalorian* mug, I choose that one.

"Excellent. I'll bring it out to you. Take a seat

anywhere you'd like."

"Where's your bathroom?" I was starting to feel like my eyeballs were floating.

"Around the corner."

I did my business and sauntered back into the main part of the café. The place was mostly deserted, aside from a couple in the darkened corner, and another couple sitting by the door I'd missed when I entered. There was a vacant table by the window, so I beelined for it, not that I needed to. Who was I competing against?

Laughing at the absurdity, I shrugged off my coat and hung it on the back of the other chair, loosening my scarf as I sat and stared. The view was fantastic, even if the falling snow was heavy enough to obscure from seeing too far down the street.

As the saying goes, wherever I was, I wasn't in Kansas anymore.

Resting my elbows on the table and steadying myself against the tiny wobble, I grabbed my phone and took a couple of pictures of both the inside of the Coffee Loft and the view outside.

Unable to stand the small tipping on the table, I rooted through my purse and found a tiny wedge, kicking it under the table leg to stop the wiggle. Secure with the stability, I nodded at the barista walking in my direction.

The young man set my devilishly delightful donut down along with my lofty-sized coffee. "If you need anything else, just let me know."

"Thank you."

I scrolled through my personal social media accounts wondering if I should post about my daily predicament. Rather than vague-booking, which I despised with every fiber of my being, I decided against telling my 188 personal friends, wait, 187, of what had transpired today. Wondering why the change in numbers, I flipped through my friend list and slumped when I noticed Gerry was missing. That didn't take long, and two can play that game.

Rolling my eyes, I went and deleted the two photos of us together; both at a Baker-Bloom work function. Just like that, he was gone. Wow.

As I went to flip my phone down, a text buzzed in from Amanda, my best friend.

Short, simple, and always to the point. *What's going on?*

I texted back. *Having a bad day. I'll tell you about it later. Promise.*

I'll come hang with you. Where are you?

No idea, but I just want to be alone. For now.

You don't know where you are?

I took a picture of the donut and the macchiato in the Baby Yoda mug with the street slightly fuzzy in the background – the falling snow helped more than the camera setting – and sent it to Amanda.

Having a chocolate day.

Dang, girl. That looks good. Bring me one.

Will do.

For fun, I posted the same picture on Instagram with #weirdwednesday and laughed loudly, covering my mouth, and apologizing when the barista looked in my direction.

As I drank my delicious caramel-infused coffee and picked at the donut, which was decidedly too sweet, I scrolled through my bank account and then through LinkedIn, searching for a new job. The bank account confirmed what I already knew – I didn't have much time to sit around. I ordered another coffee and started to feel energized and expanded my search to browse through the listings on Indeed. Nothing caught my eye.

Leg bouncing, I set the second empty cup onto the saucer, and decided it was time to head home before the snowstorm worsened. At least now I had enough caffeine in my veins to propel me easily..

I flagged the barista. "I'll clear up my bill please."

From out behind the counter, he walked in my direction, tapping my total onto the handheld unit.

Clicking on my phone, I opened Apple Pay and tapped the card reader. A loud ding, followed by the word *declined*.

"There's lots of room still," I said more to myself than the young man.

Without any expression, he punched in the total again and held the machine up for me.

Once again, I tapped, and once again I saw the dreaded word.

"It's fine, don't worry. I'll try another card. It's not your fault, something's up with the bank. I'll deal with them tomorrow. Let me try another."

I tried with the debit card, and still the transaction wouldn't go through. Embers of anger were flaring in my gut, along with a thick layer of embarrassment. I've never had failed payment transactions.

Then it hit me.

I had Baker-Bloom cards on my phone since all my transactions were work-related, but they must've cut those off, and rightly so. Dang. Stupidly, my cards hadn't been added. Double dang. I opened my tiny handbag, but my wallet – the one with my personal cards – wasn't in there. No, they were at home because today was a workday, and I was out doing work things.

Triple dang.

I rooted through my bag, finding the odd coin, but not enough. In a full panic, I flipped the bag on the table, spilling the limited contents out, magically hoping a twenty would appear between the lipstick and the dental floss, and I could leave with a tail tucked between my legs. No dice.

I swallowed. What was I going to do?

"Can I e-Transfer you?" At least I could access my bank account through the app.

Finally, there was some expression on the young man's face, which followed a shrug. "Let me ask the manager."

I scooped the scattered items and dropped them back into my purse, and heart beating loudly in my chest for anyone in eyesight to hear, stared in the direction of where the barista disappeared. Surely, an e-Transfer would be fine. Who wouldn't accept that? It was still payment.

I opened my banking app and started setting up the transfer, including a hefty tip to cover my embarrassment and any additional fees. All I needed was the email address, and I could be on my *tail-tucked-between-my-legs* way.

"I'll come out and talk to her." The voice was oddly familiar, even though it shouldn't have been. Not out here, wherever *here* was.

Turning my head, my heart stopped its incessant pounding when the six-foot one-inch Scandinavian with broad shoulders walked into the immediate area.

"Holy, wow. Cara Gallagher, is it really you?"

What the what?

Chapter Two

CARTER CROSS. The three syllables had barely finished rolling across the forefront of my brain when he stepped around the counter and strutted over in my direction.

I rose and extended my hand in a professional greeting, preferring that to the hug I sensed I was about to receive. "Hey, it's been a hot minute, hasn't it?"

One quick look to my outstretched hand and he stopped encroaching on my personal space, shaking with a firm but pleasant grip. "It's been a… a few years. How are you? You look…" A hot, sweeping gaze roamed up and down my body before he settled back to hold me in his gaze. "Wow, you look amazing, Cara."

My eyes scanned him as quickly as I could without it being weird because despite the passage of years, he looked amazing – slightly older, and yet, still the same; tall, broad shoulders, blond hair, with the addition of a well-maintained beard. The only thing missing was the playful sparkle in his dark-brown eyes. Guess we all lost that at some point.

I pushed my shoulders back and planted on a smile, falsifying my confidence. "Normally, I'm good, but I'm having quite the day. There's some kind of issue with the bank and my cards aren't working. I can e-transfer you the total if you give me the email address."

"Don't worry about it. Honestly." He waved a hand through the air. "I've got this, Harry, thank you, you can go back to the counter."

I glanced over Carter's shoulders to the young man, who with a quick nod and a *yes, sir* scurried out of earshot. Thrums of energy coursed through my fingertips as I tightened my grip on my phone, but I blamed the coffee.

"No way. I pay my own way."

A hard and fast rule I never broke. Never.

"Cara, it's good. One customer won't break the bank. Could you imagine?" He tipped his head back

22

and a low, throaty giggle escaped.

Well, hot dang, his laugh hadn't changed either and the sound still had the power to fire me up from the inside, and with it, came the strange ability to also set me at ease, as if he had some kind of power over my moods. Didn't I wish?

Guess that's why when he chose a different path than the one we were on, it sent me in a tail spin, and my being back in his presence was bad news. He had been my kryptonite, and if I didn't leave soon, I was in big trouble. And I was still upset.

"Really, can't I just transfer you the money?" My hands flew through the air; the double espresso was making me vibrate.

"No." He tipped his head to the side and stared past my eyes into the depths of my soul. It was all too easy for him to access. "Everything okay?"

I swallowed and shifted on my heeled boots, which lifted me to chin-height with him, but I turned away. "I'm just having a bad day, and this is the icing on the cake."

"Well, hopefully, it's the sweet, delicious part, and nothing bitter."

The soothing sound of his voice drew my gaze back to him. "No, this place is delightful. I enjoyed my donut and double macchiatos."

I rocked on my feet. Was it the espresso shots causing a hum inside my head, or was it all Carter? At this point, it was hard to tell.

"But if I'm honest, I really don't like being comped. That leaves more of a bitter taste in my mouth than any bad coffee ever could." My finger tapped against the edge of my phone in a wild and weird pattern.

"Well, that's an easy problem to solve." He cleared his throat, a habit I guessed he never grew out of, and sauntered back behind the counter, pulling out his wallet. After tapping on the screen, he inserted a twenty into the cash register. With an easy-going smile on his face, he winked. "Hope you don't mind, but I left a healthy tip for Harry. And now it's not comped."

Heat exploded across my face faster than ever and I took a few tentative steps forward, unsure of what to do or who to look at. Rather than check out either guy standing there, I let my gaze wander across the hardwood floor.

"Thank you, Carter. You didn't need to." The words were stronger than I felt, and my shoulders mirrored that.

"Seriously, it's all taken care of." He came over

from behind the counter and stood exceptionally close. "You're not okay, are you?"

I sighed and breathed him in – every sweet and java-scented molecule – before I stomped my foot down like a petulant child. "Just having an incredibly bad day, and I hate how you've paid the bill for me."

"Yeah, I can see that, but it's all good." The blond hairs on his taunt forearm shimmered under the glow of the lights. It wasn't helping the situation at all, and it most certainly wasn't working to keep those resurfacing feelings at bay. Not at all.

"It's not."

"Cara, I own this store. I assure you, it's all good." He cleared his throat as his thick lips pushed together. "Come over here." He gently tugged me back to my window seat and motioned for me to sit down. "What's bothering you? I know you well enough to know when something's not right."

I sat and crossed my legs, leaning back against the metal ladder frame. "You *used to* know me."

He clasped his hands together, nodded, and released a huge expulsion of air. "Yes, it's been many years, but some things don't change. You're bugged. Clearly."

My life wasn't an open book, not anymore, and

most certainly not with Carter Cross, who sat across from me like an ocean hadn't kept us apart for years.

A family walked by below on the street with a young child swinging between his parents until his boot flew off. The mother's gasp was practically audible inside the Coffee Loft.

"What is this place?" I watched as she put the boot back on, laughing and kissing the tip of her kid's nose.

"It's a coffee shop." The words were twisted in sarcasm and confusion.

I raised a meticulous eyebrow when I refocused on him. "I know that. I mean where am I?"

"I'd say lost and confused."

Yeah, some things never changed. Sarcasm had been Carter's second language. "I mean, this place, this town."

He leaned forward and narrowed his eyes. His mouth opened and closed before he finally decided to speak.

"You know what, never mind. I'll look it up myself."

Before I could unlock my phone, he placed his rough hand over mine, and talked in such an even tone I was instantly transfixed. "This is Ridge Heights, about an hour west of Rocky Mountain

House, roughly thirty-two minutes east of Cline River, which is a great place for a picnic lunch. If you keep following the highway westward, you'll come to a junction; the north takes you toward Jasper, and choosing the southbound road will take you to Banff. Both are roughly two and a half hours from here."

"Thank you. That helps."

There was no movement from his hand, or any sense of indecision about it being there in the first place, and rather than fight it, I embraced the warm touch. It was what I needed.

"You honestly had no idea where you were?"

My gaze lingered on his hand, travelling over his exposed forearm, across his perfectly pressed shirt, stopping briefly on his full lips before I settled on his dark-brown eyes. "It's been an incredibly long day, and I got in my car and just drove until I didn't want to anymore." He didn't need to know I'd screamed for part of the drive too. "I didn't notice where I was when I stopped."

A gentle snort filled the space. "That's... wow. That's a rough day."

I huffed and folded under the concerning weight of his compassionate stare. "You have no idea but thank you for your kindness and your hospitality in paying my bill, but I really should get going."

"Where are you parked?"

My lips puckered into a questionable pout and a soft sigh met my shrug. "Honestly, I have no idea." I rose and gathered my belongings. "But I'll find it."

"You're just going to wander around town in hopes of discovering it on some off chance? I know the town isn't that big, but it's big enough."

"No," I said smugly, and opened my car's app, looking to see where it was parked.

He craned his neck over to look. "What kind of car do you drive that has an app?"

"Tesla, Model 3." A gift I bought for myself after I passed my probation period at Baker-Bloom.

"Ah, fancy." A familiar expression briefly crossed his face.

I'd seen it before. When I mentioned to people what I drove, they'd immediately judged me, assuming I was haughty and better than everyone else which simply wasn't true. I'd researched for a long time before buying the car and it just made better sense for me.

Ignoring the subtle curious expression Carter tried to hide, I gave my attention to the app. "And now I know where I need to go."

Those beautiful browns of his widened, and I remembered the first time I looked at the car's app, mine had done the same. "Can't you just summon your car to come to you? Isn't that what a Tesla is all about?"

"It's an electric car, not the Batmobile." But the thought made me smile. It bore some similarities to the famous car, but not that particular feature.

"Let's see where you are again?" I showed him the app. "That's a bit of a hike. Especially in those." His gaze fell to my heeled boots.

"Well, I walked here just fine in them."

"Like what, an hour ago? Before the snow fell?"

"There was some snow falling." I empathised *some*.

A charming yet questioning expression caused his left eyebrow to rise to new heights. "Do you have good grips on them?"

There wasn't. They weren't practical walking boots; they were pretty, looked fantastic with my pants, and gave my average height a regal boost.

"Tell you what. I could use some fresh air. Let me get my jacket, and I'll be right back."

"I'm capable of walking, Carter."

"You'll slip and slide in these conditions, and truth be told," he stepped impossibly close and lowered his voice, "our hospital isn't the best, and you don't want to spend any time there. Trust me on this." He patted my arm and with a spring in his step, disappeared down the short hall.

Guess I was walking with Carter.

He returned in a heartbeat in a long, mid-thigh red and black puffer jacket, combined with a red and white toque with Canada lettered across the middle – he looked like one of our Olympic athletes. Gloves on, he pointed toward the door.

"I'll be back in a jiffy, Harry." He gave his staff a quick wave and opened the door for me. "Ladies first and watch your step. Looks like I'll need to sand this when I get back."

I death-gripped the black metal railing as I descended the seven steps to the sidewalk, which was now covered in a healthy layer of slush, but it didn't look overly slippery. Yet. The sky darkened as fast as the sun dipped behind the mountains, increasing the chill in the air.

"Which way?" I wanted to get back to my warming car as fast as possible.

"Let's see where you are parked again?"

Removing my glove, I unlocked my phone and

pointed it in his direction.

"Ah, okay, I see. You're over by Jillian's place." He cleared his throat.

"A girlfriend's house?" I didn't mean for it to be inquisitive in tone. It wasn't any of my business. It never had been, and that had been the problem.

He didn't respond to my tone and led the way down the street. "No, Jillian's is a mishmash of all things, like he's not quite sure what he wanted to sell, so he sells it all. Run by a big bouncer-type of guy named Randall. Whatever you need, like for say, you are interested in purple pompom socks, he's the guy to see."

"What?" My eyes bugged out, surprised he remembered our conversation.

"Just kidding," he laughed, "at least about him selling *purple pompom socks*. That I'd have no idea about."

It had been more of a statement than anything else, but when we were dating, I constantly complained about how much I wanted a pair of pompom socks like my much older cousin wore, but in purple, and how despite my desperate searches, I was unable to locate a pair.

"I can't believe you remembered." I gently pushed him in jest, and then death-gripped his arm when my right foot slid out a little.

Carter had stifled his sweet smile and looped an arm around my waist to steady me. "All good now?"

I stopped slipping and stared into his eyes. A slight twinkle appeared, but just as quickly disappeared. I broke the connection and focused on putting one foot in front of the other. "So tell me, what have you been up to since... Well, since the last time we..."

He released his physical hold on me and matched me step for painfully slow step. "I had big dreams to obtain an engineering degree, but halfway through my third year, when I was in Europe, I needed to stop."

I waited for a non-existent explanation. That had been when we'd broken up – our third year of post-secondary.

Focusing back on the sidewalk, he lowered his voice and shrugged. "I had a change of heart. I didn't choose the mug life; the mug life chose me."

"What?" My head tipped to the side.

"Sorry, bad pun." He let it hang in the air for a second. "I serve coffee in mugs, the mug life?"

"Oh, I get it." It was a bad pun, but had I been reading between the lines, I would've gotten it first off. "Sorry. Continue on about your dreams."

"Since everything had changed, I took some of my savings, and when the time was right, I ventured out into the world. I tried new things, I saw new places, and I pushed every last boundary I'd set my sights on."

"Oh wow." I slipped again and instinctively reached out for him.

"I got you." He offered me the crook of his arm once I was stable.

I debated – briefly – just walking in my stocking feet as I'd likely have a better grip, however, then I'd lose my toes to frostbite which wasn't any better. Instead, I gazed into Carter's eyes and whispered thanks.

"Keep telling me about your travels." I shivered in the cool breeze.

"Well, I was in this place in South America and went on a coffee bean tour as a why not kind of expedition, and it turned out I was fascinated by the process. Of how they treat the workers, of how it all got done, everything. For a week after, since I had nowhere to go, I volunteered my services and helped harvest the cherries."

"Cherries? Really?" Now I knew I was being played. Coffee came from beans, not cherries.

"Seriously." He nodded and slowed his pace a touch. "They aren't the red cherries you and I are used to from the BC interior, but I learned which cherries were ripe for picking and we hand-harvested those. Then we spread them in the sun to dry. I wasn't there for the rest, but my friend, Diego, informed me how they dry out for a few weeks until they are at the right moisture content, and then they are sold to millers."

I wanted to doubt the veracity of his story, but one look at his face to see the sincerity in the way his lips curled up and the corners of his eyes smiled as he spoke with fondness.

"You really went to harvest coffee?" It was mind-blowing.

"I did. I loved it so much when I came home, I took a job at a coffee shop. But I learned I didn't just want a good cup of coffee; I needed a *great* cup of coffee. So I researched more, visited other plantations, and learned about the coffee-making process."

"Geez, Carter, I'm impressed."

We passed a section of stores with large canvas awnings, and surprisingly the further we ambled down the street, the more the traffic picked up. The Coffee Loft must be in the quieter section of town.

"Want to hear something even more interesting?"

"Of course." I leaned in closer.

"Did you know the workers haul, on average, between 100 and 200 pounds of cherries a day, and of that, only twenty to forty pounds of coffee beans are produced? The workers get paid based on the merit of their daily work, and it's incredibly hard work." He shook his head which threw our stepping off.

"That's actually, that's pretty cool. After that, and getting a barista job, you decided to manage a shop?"

"Yes, and no. After hearing how the plantation workers are treated, some sadly aren't treated well, I went back to school and got a business degree instead."

"Oh, I bet your parents were happy."

Once upon a time, the Cross family had big dreams for their engineer son, especially since his sisters hadn't done much with their lives, or at least the last time I'd seen them they hadn't.

"Ah, whatever. They learned to live with it. Money isn't everything and it only gets you so far."

I shrugged. Maybe it wasn't, but it sure helped to take the edge off. "And then what did you do?"

He slowed again to match my pace. "I bought this place and am working on producing the best dang coffee north of Columbia, all the way back to how the cherries are grown until the beans land in my shop and I grind them to perfection. Part of my plan is to pay the workers more, treat them well, and move it up the chain. Ideally, I'd love all the Coffee Lofts on board, with the money feeding back to the workers." He shook his head. "I don't need a fancy car or a second home, but they need a solid roof over their head, food on their table, and better working conditions."

"Wow, Carter, I'm impressed." Such a change from the guy who *was* going to own fancy cars and have at least two homes, one of which was someplace warmer than the middle of Alberta.

He kept his focus ahead of us. "We'll need to walk down this way."

I held tight as we stepped onto the road and crossed over it. "And you're happy?"

He faced me, his gaze dancing over my face. "For the most part, yeah. If I can succeed with that, then at least I can say I did something good for the world. That would make me happy. Truly happy."

"Your wife and kids must be thrilled and your biggest supporters." I hadn't chanced a look at his ring finger, not that it meant anything these days. Cheaters wore rings and some married men did not. Sadly, I could no longer trust what the ring finger portrayed.

He snorted and then laughed. "Yeah, no wife, and definitely no kids. The last girlfriend pretty much sealed the deal on never wanting to procreate or get married."

"Piece of work, was she?"

"Remember Rachel Rose?"

"Our high-school valedictorian?" Who was as snobbish as they came, drop-dead gorgeous but wow, what a witch especially if you weren't part of her callous cliquey crowd.

Carter nodded, cresting his brow up into his hairline.

"No way."

"Multiplied by ten."

"Why'd you ever go out with that kind of mess then?"

He shrugged, and it tugged on my arm. "Desperation, I suppose. I've never quite figured out the why either. Superficial perhaps, as maybe I was just at a low point and needed someone who would boost my self-confidence." There was no eye contact as his voice fell. "This you?"

I spotted my car. "What gave it away?"

"Ridge Heights isn't known for its high volume of Teslas."

"I take it there's no charging station here either?" The battery was low, but not dangerously low.

He shook his head. "Nope. Not for miles. You may get lucky in Nordegg, or Rocky Mountain House if you're heading east."

"I'll look into the app and see what I can find." I opened the car door and reached for the like-new snow brush.

He took it from my hands and started clearing my car. "You warm it up, and I'll brush it off."

"She's already running."

"Well, I'll be floored."

He swept off the windshield and the roof, as I walked over to the passenger side and opened his door.

"I'll give you a ride back and give you a quick mini-tour so the next time someone mentions a Tesla, you won't mistake it for the Batmobile." I winked as I climbed into the warm interior.

Carter joined me a moment later, setting the snowbrush on the passenger floorboards. He snuggled against the seat and whistled. "This is a sweet ride."

"Thanks." I pointed out a couple of the cooler in-car features. "Casper is the best car I've had."

"Casper? You named your car after the movie ghost?" There was an unmistakable smirk brewing, and it was spreading to his eyes. It was nice to see a sparkle returning, even if briefly.

However, a fresh flashing of heat, unrelated to the vehicle warming, bloomed across my cheeks. "My car is white, and I have fond memories of the friendly ghost, so yeah, it just fit."

A lazy smile stretched across his face. "Yeah, fond memories."

Years ago, needing a mental break from all life was throwing at us, we attended a midnight showing of classic 90s movies, and Casper the Friendly Ghost was playing. As a fresh couple, flirting with all new ideas, we attended. It was our third date, and after the movie ended, it was the first time we kissed.

Now here we were many years after that first kiss.

Remembering the reason for the breakup came from him, the ghostly tentacles of achy pain spread through my chest as I put the car in gear and headed back in the direction of the Coffee Loft. The air around us chilled, and the interior was as quiet as the car trudging down the main street.

Eventually, I found a spot outside the shop, and I pulled into it like a perfect professional parker. The autopark certainly helped.

"Thanks for the ride back." He put his hand on the door and was searching for the handle.

"Push this button down." I reached across and showed him, causing him to jump back a little. "It lowers the windows before you open."

"Cool beans." His hand lingered on the door's armrest.

"Thanks again for paying my bill. I promise to pay you back."

"It's all good, Cara. I swear." He pushed the door fully open and climbed out to stand on the sidewalk. "If you're ever in this part of the world again, pop in and say hi. It's nice to see a friendly face."

"And if you're ever in the Red Deer area, look me up." Somehow, someway.

"Will do." He straightened himself up and stretched, giving me a quick peek at what was once his wall of abs. "Oh, hey." He popped his head back into the interior. "I know Ridge Heights is a bit of a drive, but..." A snowflake swirled into the interior as Carter's words froze in his lungs. Swallowing, he inhaled and tried again. "What would you say to meeting for dinner on the weekend?"

I pursed my lips together, picking and choosing the right words to say, but he interrupted my thoughts.

"Holy beans, I never thought to ask. You have a husband and a family, don't you?"

I shook my head and avoided eye contact. "Nope, I'm as single as they come but it's just not the right time. Sorry."

"Then it wasn't meant to be. Take care."

He closed the door and scaled the steps back into his shop.

Was I the world's biggest idiot, or just in this neck of the woods? Was I being given a second chance, and rather than accept it, I had to have been certifiable to drive away, yet that's exactly what I did. However, I kept glancing in the rearview mirror because life was funny that way.

Chapter Three

"OKAY, WHAT?" AMANDA stretched out on her foam mat for our morning Pilates class. "Run that all by me again."

"The short and sweet version is I got canned and dumped within a five-minute span and ran into an old boyfriend a couple of hours later in a place I shouldn't have been in to begin with."

In the open area of my living room, where we worked through a Pilates app off her phone, she pressed her shoulders and feet flat into the ground and lifted her abs into the sky, holding them tightly. I followed but dropped my butt back onto the mat before she did.

"And who was this guy again?" She lifted once more.

"From college."

"And you... broke up... when..."

"Start of our third year. He accepted an offer overseas while I went to the U of C. Although we agreed to separate, it had been his suggestion. After a while, I stopped thinking about him." I tried to mirror Amanda's form and struggled to hold myself up for any length of time. Getting back into shape was brutal.

Amanda seemed to have hit her zone as she appeared peaceful and wasn't struggling to stay lifted or even catch her breath. She repeated the exercise, doing twice as many as I did. At least when we did our evening walks, I could dominate her in speed, but the Pilates part was killing me.

I stayed firmly at my back, arms touching my hips, and stared up at my non-descript ceiling. I didn't want to talk about Carter, who had been an uninvited yet most welcomed guest to my dreams last night. "Oh, yeah, and the jerks cancelled my cards—"

"As they should've."

"Right but maybe they should've given me a heads up."

"Or maybe you should've had your personal cards added to your Apple Pay to have prevented such a scene."

"I didn't cause a scene." Because that wasn't me anymore.

"Except you said the manager came out." She lowered down and rolled onto her hip, challenging me to debate my point.

"The old flame *was* the manager."

"Ooh, you missed that part because I thought you said he went to college."

"He did."

"Coffee store managers go to college?"

"Why wouldn't they?" My eyes narrowed, and my brow furrowed.

"You'll have wrinkles before your forties if you keep making that face."

"That is my face. Nothing I can do to change that."

Effortlessly, she rolled onto her back and performed a few sets of scissors.

"The point being is I was highly embarrassed, and I'd already had a terrible day."

"And the manager came to your rescue. How sweet."

I wanted to toss a throw pillow at her, but there were none available within easy reach, so I did the next best thing and tossed a stretchy band. I should've stretched it out like an elastic band first, it would've had a greater impact.

"So what, big deal."

"You're saying it's not a big deal how I lost my job and my boyfriend?" I waited until she finished her reps and joined her as we moved into the next position – leg circles. When this ten-week app finished, I'd better have stronger abs.

With nary a grunt, Amanda lifted her right leg into the air and made several circles. "That's not what I'm saying at all. I'm saying it's no big deal that you were embarrassed at the coffee place. I'm sure it happens all the time, and if he was an old boyfriend like you said he was, he was probably more than willing to help you out."

"That's the problem. He had zero issue with it, and now I owe him one." I grunted as I moved my left leg into the air.

Amanda switched legs. "You don't owe him anything. Did he say you had to pay him back?"

"No. But it's out in the universe. These things have a way of working themselves out."

"Yes, karma does have that effect, but you don't owe him. If he was clear he was good, you need to let it go."

Let it go. Something I wasn't very good at.

Actually, scratch that, very good implied I could let things go. I never let anything go. Old wounds festered for years. I had a nasty habit of remembering every bad thing that had ever happened, and not letting anyone around me forget how *I* hadn't forgotten. Amanda should've known that.

"Listen, if it's that big a deal to you go back there and pay for it then all will be right within your world again." She rolled into a sitting position. "This is not a difficult situation to fix. In fact, this is easy."

"Oh really?" I rolled my eyes which was easier than getting into a sitting position. "If your old fling, what was his name again, oh right, Jordan, if he was to take care of a bill for you because you suddenly were unable to, you'd totally be okay with it?" Hah.

However, voicing it made me sound like a witch, which proved how much I was, but it was out of line. The pained expression ghosting across her freckled face sent a deep ache to my soul, and I hated myself for having inflicted any kind of hurt on my best friend.

Things between Amanda and Jordan went disastrously wrong, and I was the worst friend in the world to have brought up his name. That jerk would've gloated and paraded around like he was some kind of saviour if he had come to her rescue.

"I'm sorry. That was uncalled for." I reached for her hand, and the softest, most sincere voice breathed out of me. Tears built up and threatened to break free of the dam.

She inhaled and pushed herself to a standing position, extending a hand to help me up. "It was, but you made your point." Locking her sights on me, she nodded. "You're right, when you put it that way, it would be a big deal."

"Thank you. That was all the acknowledgment I needed; I just had a terrible way of demonstrating my side."

"You'd suck in a debate match."

"No doubt about that." I rolled up my mat and tucked it into my corner of pipe dreams which also included a small weight set, a jump rope, and a stretch band.

"You're done? Already?"

"Yeah, my heart isn't in it today. Figure I'll just add an extra kilometre on my walk to make up for it."

"You know what? I agree. I'm not feeling this today either."

"Besides, you already look amazing."

And she honestly did. Amanda was a perfect size six or eight, depending on the brand she wore, and she worked hard to maintain her figure. It appeared effortless, but there was a lot of investment. Reasonable portions, no calorie-laden drinks (except for the occasional glass of wine), and no licks, bites, or tastes of food. Three meals and two snacks daily, a ritual she did not budge from.

I, on the other hand, worked hard at eating the wrong things and not giving two cares about how I appeared to others. Once upon a time, like in my early teens, I was a svelte size six, but I wasn't as happy as I was being a size ten. A girl needed to live a little. Or a lot on the weekends.

In the kitchen, I poured a couple of mugs of coffee and pulled out two prepackaged muffins.

Amanda sat at the bar-height table and crossed her legs as I sat down our breakfast. "So tell me about Carter, is he cute? Wait, first, is he single?"

I rolled my eyes, although it was a warranted question. "Yes."

"Good, best place to start. And he's a business owner, so that makes him smart."

I climbed onto the chair and picked the crumbly top part off my muffin; always the tastiest bit. "He's super passionate about how coffee is produced."

"That's a weird thing to be excited about." She scrunched up her perfect upturned nose and then popped a chunk of muffin into her mouth.

"Actually, it was neat to hear the energy in his voice though since he lost his zest. As did I." All it took was one life-changing moment to seal the deal. "However, he used to have this amazing sparkle in his eyes, the kind that lit up when he used to see me, and that was gone too. But for a moment, it returned."

"Times are tough. Things have changed. Everyone's working harder but not necessarily being blessed with a raise to help with the nasty rising costs of inflation, so it's a good thing his business is still going strong. It's a tough world out there."

"I know." I glanced at my friend. "He seems different, yet still the same in many ways, but different."

"Like you?" An all-knowing expression filled her face.

I tossed my gaze to the steaming coffee watching as heated air currents rose from my mug. "Yeah, like me."

"Even in the few years I've known you, time's hardened you. I'm sure it's changed him too. It did a number on me as well."

I scoffed. Amanda was like a phoenix; she rose through her trauma and became better and stronger than she had been before. Letting go of things was her greatest strength and aside from the jerk, she never let things weigh her down. I envied that about her.

After a sip, I set the coffee down and rubbed my thumb across to catch the runoff. "Growing up bites. Do you ever wish you could go back in time and just be twenty again?"

"No!" Her hands smacked the table before I'd barely finished my question. "Absolutely no. Working full-time while also in school, and trying to find time to eat yet still pay the bills? No, thank you. I much prefer having a steady job with long hours, but at least I'm working. I'm not worried about my finances, my debt is diminishing, and I still get out. A lot. The dating pool is also better at this age. I can weed out the losers, and maybe one day, I'll actually pick the winner."

"Things aren't working out with Kevin?"

She cast her gaze down and with the tip of her finger, flicked out a piece of apple from her muffin. "He's a nice enough guy but he's missing something. I just can't figure out what."

"Chemistry?"

She snorted and tossed her long dark hair over her shoulder. "Probably, even though he's everything I thought I wanted - stable, single, and treats me well, but it's meh."

Meh. The mere word lit up the metaphorical lightbulb. Is that what Gerry thought of me? Was I meh to him? He'd often said I was everything he wanted, and things were going so well between us, so where did it all go wrong?

Maybe if I had been a better girlfriend or remembered every single detail of information he shared with me, he'd still be around? But it wasn't like I didn't care, quite the contrary. My mind was just constantly filled with a million plus one things I needed to do every day to keep my head above water, so perhaps a conversation or two slipped through. Yes, maybe I should've paid attention and done the things he wanted to do.

I paused, reflecting on my words.

Good grief, maybe it wasn't a conversation slipping through, maybe it was the entirety of our relationship. Like a dying plant, I hadn't given it enough water, and it could only hold out for so long before giving up.

Oh, for Pete's sake.

I had been a terrible girlfriend.

Amanda's eyes widened and a deeply concerned look shadowed her otherwise chipper expression. "You're that upset about the breakup with Gerry?"

I shook my head because it wasn't the truth – I wasn't completely upset. It was weird to think it was more the idea of Gerry I missed because apparently there hadn't been much to the relationship considering how I wasn't great girlfriend material and all that. Still…

My vision blurred the tiniest bit, but it was easy enough to reign it back.

"Oh, Honey, there ain't no man on Earth worth crying over."

I swiped at my eyes; thankful the dampness hadn't broken free. "I swear it's not tears; it's sweat." I fanned my shirt and looked anywhere but at the sympathetic smile tugging on my best friend's lips. "It's quite warm in here, isn't it?"

"Sure, warm. Mmhmm."

Gerry and I had been together for six months and had talked about him shifting into more serious territory. Eventually. But it never happened, and now he was gone. Was I truly that upset over him ditching me? I didn't think I was because I hadn't cried over a breakup since… well, since Carter.

AFTER AMANDA WENT home to ready for another day at the law offices of Skye Fox & Thorne, I scrolled the job listings, coming up empty. Nothing struck a chord, and nothing even remotely sounded interesting. Everything was – to use Amanda's brilliant word – meh.

Giving up for the time being, I deleted my work cards from Apple Pay and smartly added my own before adding every other points card I had floating in the hallows of my purse. Once I was sure I had everything inputted correctly, I grabbed my laptop and some cash as it was time to pay off a debt. And maybe see Carter again. Especially since I hadn't been able to stop thinking about him.

Before I stepped out of my apartment, I stopped in front of an old picture of my father and six-year-old me standing in front of his business – Gallagher's Sporting Goods. He'd been so proud of his shop and worked there daily until he, on a whim and a prayer, decided he wanted a break in the business and sold it.

Not long after that, he dropped the bomb about his terminal cancer diagnosis. That was five years ago. It hadn't been a whim and a prayer, he'd known, and being the amazing dad he was, he didn't want me to have to deal with his business after his passing.

I stared at the picture again, seeing the deepened wrinkles in the corners of his grey-blue eyes, the lopsided smile, and the nicks on the fingertips of his hands upon my shoulders. Despite the many times he'd asked me to look at the camera, I couldn't stop looking up at him, and in this snapshot, his head was tipped down in my direction not hiding his boisterous grin. Once upon a time, he'd shown me the takes, but of them all, this was the picture he'd chosen to hang behind the order desk because it was real, and you could sense the emotion within.

Dang, I had so many fond memories of hanging out and working in his shop, and of using the tools and creating something with my bare hands. Best of all, I'd gotten to hang out with my dad, sing old Johnny Cash songs when the customers weren't around, and watch him do what he loved. We weren't close in the sense we shared our secrets or anything, but we could count on each other. Always.

It was the best of times. And grief was the absolute worst.

"I'm figuring some things out, Dad, but don't you worry. I'll get it handled, and I won't eat up my savings before I do. You have my word; however, I will welcome any advice or signs or whatever you can send my way." I placed a fingertip kiss on his head and bid him adieu.

A while later, I parked on the next street over from the Coffee Loft and headed inside. There was an unmistakable rich chocolate aroma in the air that instantly had me salivating.

I recognized Harry upon approach, but I was pretty sure I wasn't familiar to him. At least he acted like I wasn't.

"Good afternoon, what can I get you?"

"Whatever is being whipped up currently. I could smell the heavenly scent outside."

"That's our Muddy Pie. It's a donut with a chocolate cookie crumble glaze, stuffed with a decadent vanilla cream, and topped with crushed cookies." His voice cracked on the last word, and he covered his mouth.

Thank goodness Amanda and I had a long walk planned. I'd need it after what I was about to order.

"I'll have one of those please, plus a mug of Coffee Loft's dark roast. In a lofty size," I added for good measure. One sweet baked item would cure my craving, didn't need to add a sugar-laden drink to my order as well.

"Yes, ma'am. Please have a seat, and I'll bring it out to you."

Seeing the window table was vacant, I rushed over and sat in what I was going to lovingly call *my spot*, preferring to people watch on the main street; a couple passed by a lady with a giant, blonde-haired dog, and a couple of giggling teens snickered together.

The sidewalks were free of snow and ice but that didn't reduce the chill in the air. Like it or not, autumn was in full bloom and winter was nipping at her heels.

My hot drink arrived tantalizing my senses with its ripe java scent, as did my ten-pound gaining donut. I picked and drank for the better part of an hour while alternating my attention on the sidewalk below and the job search in front of me.

I just wasn't sure I had the energy to complete online forms, and fill out necessary paperwork, and brag about my achievements, which were few and far between. How was I supposed to make myself look like someone to hire when I hadn't been able to hold down a job for any length of time?

Even logging into LinkedIn didn't light a fire under me. It sucked having to update my work status. Again.

From the corner of my eye, I spied Carter, dressed in a nice button-up, wearing a Coffee Loft brown apron wrapped around his chest and waist and tied in the front. He was walking around with a tray holding a bunch of tiny mugs and stopped at each table, the muscles tensing in his bare forearms, before eventually making his rounds over to me.

"Good evening. Fancy meeting you in a place like this." He was all smiles. Gorgeous, mega-watt smiles pushed up the corners of his eyes, which sadly, still lacked his once familiar sparkle.

"Hey." I tried my best to not give in to my personal kryptonite. Carter and his casual conversations weren't what I needed.

"I'm handing out samples of a new brew I've blended. Care to try?" He set the tray down and offered me a sample-sized mug. "You don't have to try it in my presence, but here's a comment card if you don't mind filling out a brief survey." He put a golf-style pencil atop the card and took a step away.

"Where are you going? There's no need to rush away, I'll try it now." I lifted the mug to my lips and allowed a small taste to wash over my tastebuds. Remembering how Amanda talked about her wine tastings, I did my best to mimic the movement and let the savoury taste of the warm coffee sit a second or two longer than normal. "It's good."

His hand gripped the edge of the tray like he was ready to bolt. "Like good-good and you'd have another, or it's meh-good and it wouldn't be your first choice? Or is it fab-brew-lous?"

My head tipped back with a chuckle. "You're funny."

"Thanks, I try my best."

"Are you asking all your samplers that way?"

A sweet laugh filled the space. "Heavens, no. I'd be shut down but with you… I just…"

I inhaled. "Yeah." It was all I needed to say because I understood it perfectly.

"So?"

A smile snuck onto my otherwise serious face; it was impossible to keep it away. "I would definitely have another. There's no bitter aftertaste, but there is a lingering taste of something I can't quite put my finger on."

"And it's good, that lingering taste?" The curiosity was ripe on his tongue.

"Of course. It's like something familiar and soothing, but I couldn't tell you what."

I took another sip, hoping it would trigger something. Instead, all it did was remind me of sunlit Sunday mornings on a front porch with the bright colours of the autumn-touched leaves swaying in the warm breeze. Gee whiz, I needed to get out more.

"I'm not sure, but it's quite nice. Well done, it really is fab-brew-lous."

He pointed to the vacant seat. "May I sit after I've handed these out?"

"Of course. It's your shop." I winked.

With a quick nod, he delivered the remaining mugs and dropped off a handful of survey cards before he returned and sat.

"So, what brings you out this way?" Like a flash, his gaze flickered to my laptop before returning to look me in the eyes. "A little far from the big city."

Big city? It was Red Deer; a tenth of the size of the major cities north and south of me. However, comparing Ridge Heights to Red Deer was like comparing Red Deer to Calgary, so it was all in interpretation.

"It is a bit of a drive, but you know a great cup of coffee," I tapped my mug after closing the laptop. "Is worth the drive. Besides driving gives me time to think." And with this trip, I wasn't screaming my head off. A definite bonus.

"Oh yeah, what are you thinking about?"

"All the things."

"So, nothing's changed?" His smile mixed with the crinkle in his eyes, both had the ability to set me at ease. How was that possible? Especially after all these years?

I shook my head and ran my hand down the length of my ponytail, pulling the extra length over my shoulder. "I'm still the same hot mess I was back in high school and college."

"Oh, I doubt that." He leaned closer and the tray bumped into my laptop. With a quick movement, he removed it and leaned it against the wall beside him. "Don't let me forget it's there."

"I won't." I took another sip from the mug; it had an addictive taste, and my rating on it was increasing with each sip.

"Well, it's nice to see you smiling again; you always had a great smile. Last week, you looked a little rough around the edges."

A soul-crushing sigh blew out of my lungs with the weakest of effort. "Oh. My. Goodness. That was some day."

"That bad, eh? Tell me about it? People have mentioned I'm like a therapist and all it will cost you is a cup of coffee, so I'm super affordable too." Those deep eyes penetrated the crushing depths of my soul, but unlike most, he didn't turn away. He pulled up a metaphorical chair and got comfy.

I, on the other hand, did turn away as a shiver coursed through my veins, but it wasn't enough to stop me from talking, it just prevented me from making any kind of connection as I did so. "I'm getting a bit of a restart, in love and in the business world."

"Ooh, those are tough, and both at the same time? Double rough."

"I lost my job and my boyfriend within five minutes."

"That's a... wow. Within five minutes? Yikes. That's a lot to take in a short amount of time."

"And then I drove aimlessly until I somehow arrived here, ordered some refreshments, and was embarrassed beyond belief how I couldn't cover my tab." One flicker of a gaze to the questioning expression, and I buried my face into the palms of my hands. "It was a bad day."

He reached across the bistro-sized table and gave my arm a squeeze. "I'm so sorry for that day."

Slowly, I chanced a peek. He was every bit as warm and comforting as his voice led me to believe. "Thank you for helping me out of a pickle."

"That's what I'm here for."

"Speaking of…" I grabbed my purse and dug through until I found the right amount of cash and slipped it under my mug. "For the last visit."

"No way."

"It's staying there. Your good man Harry will have it for a huge tip if you don't take it."

He pinched the bridge of his nose and blinked almost as if he was in pain. After a quick breath, he carried on. "Cara, I told you before, it's all taken care of. It wasn't that big a deal."

"To you, maybe, but it was a big deal to me." I pushed the mug-stacked cash closer to him. There was no way it was going home with me.

Carter pushed it back in my direction.

I raised a brow, tipped my head at him, and flagged the barista. "Harry?"

Immediately he beelined over to the table, after first nervously glancing at his boss. "Yes, ma'am."

I cringed. "Can you ring up two caramel macchiato and one specialty donut, but not actually make them? Use this to pay for them." I stuffed the cash into his hand. "And keep what's leftover as a tip."

The Adam's Apple bobbed, and his voice squeaked. He flipped to his boss; the questioning gaze covered his pimply face. "Sir?"

"If that's what the customer wants, then I think you should do it." The look he sent me tickled a delight I hadn't felt in years. It was smug, all-knowing, and somehow electric.

"Yes, sir. Thank you, Ma'am." He scurried off behind the counter.

"I think you've made his day."

"At least someone is happy."

"Aw, I'm sure you make a lot of people happy." A faint blush coloured his cheeks as he tipped his head down and repositioned himself at the table. It took a moment or two for him to get into a comfortable position; one that lasted longer than five seconds.

"Not lately. Did you know over the last five years I've had at least twelve different jobs?"

"I did not know that."

I dug the edge of my nail into a groove on the laptop and ran it down the length. "I'm either let go because the probation period was almost over, and they felt I wasn't a right fit for their space, or I get fired, plain and simple. When I survived the probation period at the last job, I got a little excited, because you know, I'd finally made it." My laugh was ironically cold and without feeling. "So that's when I ordered Casper."

Carter tipped his head to the side.

"My car." I sighed and clasped my hands overtop the laptop.

"Right. Anyway, carry on." He waved me to continue.

"It was a nine-month wait for the colour and specs I wanted, so it arrived on my first anniversary, and honestly, things were going great. A year later, I'd even managed to hold on to a boyfriend for longer than a couple of months." Why I had to share *that* part was beyond reasonable comprehension, yet somehow it propelled me forward. "Thought I had finally made it as an adult and was starting to check off the right boxes."

"Must've been a great feeling."

I turned my focus over to him, grateful someone understood. "It was. I was on top of the world, and I was doing big things." A satisfying memory filled my soul for a brief moment. "My future seemed bright. Finally figured my dad would be proud of me."

He squinted as if the lights became too bright and he ran his fingertips over his brows. "I'm sure he is."

I shrugged but couldn't correct his tense. Carter did not know about my dad's untimely passing, and although it hurt too much to bring it up, I needed to. Back in the day, they had enjoyed each other's company.

A lack of compassion rolled out of me like a steamroller, and my voice went as dead as I felt. "Dad passed away five years ago." My head bobbled sideways back and forth as the tears built and blurred my vision. "Which I guess is a relief since he's not here to witness the giant hot mess sitting before you."

Tenderly, he grasped my hands between his and through my fuzzy vision, he slumped forward. "I knew about Benson. I was there for the funeral, and it was the worst way to spend your birthday."

How could he have been there? How would he have known about Dad's passing? Why didn't he stop and say hi?

But I couldn't voice a thing, nothing breathed out of me but pain. The lump forming rapidly in the back of my throat felt as if it was attempting to strangle me.

"You were surrounded by people constantly, and after how things were between us, I didn't want to make things awkward or anything by talking to you. But I was there, watching you, wishing there was something I could do to help you, but I'm grateful for those who stood by you as you were never alone." His shoulders rolled forward. "You wore a knee-length dress with long sleeves, and your hair was slicked back in a half pony. That day you wore your glasses, so you must've had an incredible headache, but I thought it was awesome how you wore a Gallagher's Hardware Apron. It was a cool touch."

I still couldn't believe he'd been there, and I kept blinking and breathing hard, hoping the tears wouldn't burst the dam and run free, as then I'd be in big trouble.

"Cara, I am so sorry for your loss. I adored Benson, and fishing with him was the best. He was truly a cool dude amongst men."

"He was." My voice croaked as the tears broke free and streamed down my cheeks. So much for keeping myself together.

Dad and Carter had enjoyed a couple of fishing trips back when we were together. He'd often thought of Carter as the son he never had.

Once again, Carter pinched the bridge of his nose and squinted his eyes as the colour drained from his face.

Suddenly, he seemed nervous and twitchy, unable to sit still. He scanned the dining area and rose with such a start, I jumped.

"I'm sorry. Umm, give me a minute, and I'll be right back. I just need…"

I didn't get to say anything further. I couldn't – he bolted to the office behind the counter.

What was going on?

Chapter Four

WHY WAS IT that whenever a lady cried, the men suddenly felt uncomfortable and needed to escape? All my life I've never understood that.

Drying my eyes, I waited over an hour for Carter to return to a visible position within his store, but despite the uptick in customers, he never appeared. I'd even inquired to Harry who said he was taking care of business and didn't expand further. Still, it was weird, and it left a bitter taste in my mouth.

A variety of customers came in and left, although some stayed for a brief time. It was interesting to watch and study the dynamics of it all. It was the one thing I'd been good at with Baker-Bloom, seeing the big picture after breaking it down into smaller pieces.

But it was the overheard conversation that started ideas rolling. A customer pointed out how the Coffee Loft never did fun promotions like the other places in town and rarely had deals. It was too bad, she said, because this place was charming and had so much appeal, and a huge promo would be a boon for the place.

I couldn't help but agree. The shop was steady, and not busy, but it had more downtime than up. The financials had to be enough to keep the place afloat, but what if it got a healthy boost? What if it became the spot to go when passing through?

Whenever I ventured to Banff, there was one spot I just had to stop at in Canmore. It was always factored into my schedule, as the place was bustling and the wait times just to order the fresh bagels were always twenty to thirty minutes long. The Coffee Loft could be similar. If that was what Carter wanted. Except, I didn't see him again so I could even ask.

Tired of waiting, I stopped my endless searching of both the internet and the store and called it a day. I paid my bill, and after one final glance, I scanned the nooks and crannies for him, but like vapor, he'd disappeared. As did I.

* * *

"OH MY GOODNESS, you went back?" Amanda asked as she sliced into her filet of salmon.

"You think that's wrong?" I took a sip of my water.

I would've preferred a nice glass of chardonnay to compliment the meal, but with my lack of income padding my lacklustre bank account, I needed to cut back somewhere. As it was, my two trips to the Coffee Loft had taken a chunk of disposable income away.

Amanda sized me up with her big, brown, doe-eyed look. "On the contrary, I think it's adorable. Did you do it out of guilt or out of something more?"

"Oh, it was guilt."

She lifted her fork and paused before she took a bite, raising her brow just enough to let me know she knew me better and just wanted me to vocalize it.

"Fine," I shrugged, looking over her shoulder at the busboy as he cleaned a nearby table. "It was both."

"Ooh. I like the idea of something more. A rebound. Someone to make you find the spark in life once again." She wiggled her brows.

"I have spark, Amanda." I did. It just needed a bit of polishing.

"Of course, you do. You just keep it under lock and key and never let it out. Not even when someone begs." She stuffed her mouth with a forkful of food.

"Not true."

"Really?" She swallowed and chased it with a quick sip of wine. "What was the last romantic thing you and Gerry did together? What was the last thing he did for you that made the butterflies come alive?"

Gerry was the quintessential romantic, or at least he had been when we first started dating; all flowers and mini-impromptu dates. However, Amanda had a point.

"But I don't recall ever feeling butterflies around him, he was just Gerry. A great guy. The type who gave me my space when I needed it, and was just there when I needed to share space with another person."

"Do you hear yourself when you talk?" Her eyes widened as she set her fork to the side of her plate and leaned on her forearms.

"Of course, why?"

"Gerry wasn't a boyfriend to you or for you. He

was just there like a work friend you hang out with because you have no choice. No wonder he broke up with you."

"Hey."

"Well?" The look she shot in my direction had me shrinking into my seat. She never sugar-coated a thing. It was what I liked most about her and hated at the same time.

I huffed, not liking at all where the conversation was going.

Gerry and I were a complicated mix. He'd been my favourite server at a high-end downtown restaurant, and I'd always requested his section whenever I had a work date there or when Amanda could meet me. Then I needed a date, and so I casually asked him out to a work function – where all the expenses were paid, he just needed to be there – for no other reason than to show my incorrigible boss how I had interests outside of work. Those interests were romantic because deep down I had a feeling Tory was interested in me and if I showed up with some arm candy, maybe he'd back off. It worked. Thank goodness.

Gerry became my plus-one on several occasions, and I attended the one staff function where he introduced me as his serious girlfriend. It was off-putting because it came with strings, and yet, I wasn't ready to cut the strings. I enjoyed his company; he was funny and had a certain charm about him that put most people at ease. In short, he was a good look on me and we fit well together.

Karma was laughing her face off. Like being fired from my job and then losing the shiny decoration of Gerry at the same time, as if, since I no longer had a job, I had nowhere to show a boyfriend off anymore. What a disaster.

I picked at my grilled chicken. "What now?"

"I don't know," she drawled out the words. "Actually, why don't I ask Kevin to see if one of his single friends wants to join us on a double date?"

Before she'd finished her sentence, I was already shaking my head. "How about no thanks?"

"Aw, come on. It could be fun."

"Is this your way of telling me things are getting better between you and Kevin?"

Her gaze dropped fast to her salmon. "No. But I was hoping a fresh influx of people and dating ideas would spark something."

"Still that bad, eh?"

"He's great. On paper, he's a ten. In the sack, he's a solid seven." She tipped her hand back and forth. "Maybe a seven-point-five, but still."

"But there's still no chemistry?"

She sagged into her seat. "I've tried everything I can think of, and I come up empty. There's just nothing there, and I figured maybe if we put you and one of his friends together, something will click for us."

"Maybe, but I'm not interested in dating."

"Except for Carter."

I stabbed a piece of chicken and dragged it through a string of sauce. "I'm not interested in dating him, it was just nice to see him again."

"It's almost a two-hour drive just for that pleasure." A smirk filled her face, and she pursed her lips off to one side in a knowing way.

"What?"

"That's all I'm saying about that." She popped a piece of her roll into her mouth. "So, how are things on the work front?"

"Like my dating profile – one disaster after another."

"Oh gee whiz."

"Everything I look at doesn't excite me. The job writeups are boring as all get out, and if those are bad, the job itself can't be much better."

"What about a headhunter? Or looking at a temp position?"

"I never thought about those." They were valid jumping off points. A headhunter would find me the job of my dreams, or so I was led to believe. "I'm not sure I want something temp though. I'd like something that will last—"

"Longer than a couple of years?"

"Precisely." I chewed on my chicken and scanned the restaurant.

It was full, as always. The same lunch groups were at their same tables. Everything was always the same. Nothing ever changed.

"Ever thought of opening your own marketing business? You know what you're doing, and this way you can take the clients you want, rather than being dumped with the undesirables."

I tapped my chin and pondered her idea. "It's not an awful idea."

"There you go."

"It would require a lot of a startup."

The type of cash I didn't have available and wasn't sure I'd be able to secure with my inability to hold onto a job, and there was no way I was touching my inheritance. That was for my retirement. I was going to see the world Dad had always dreamed about it. I just needed another twenty-five to thirty years until I could use it. Until then, it was sitting in an account. Waiting.

"I could fund you."

My eyes widened. "Absolutely not."

"Why not? That's what friends are for. I can loan you a small start-up to get you going."

"But…" I had no words. It was a huge offer. Bigger than huge.

"Plus, I could help on the legal side and make sure everything is legit, get a name going, start up the website, and all the fun that goes into that." Amanda lit up and started spitting out idea after idea.

It could be fun being the boss, but then again, I didn't have the first idea of how to start a business – what steps to take, although partnering with Amanda seemed like the logical first step – she had all the brightest of ideas, and best of all, it sounded like a logical plan.

All I knew was how pricey it would be to get it off the ground, and although I had access to a fairly healthy nest egg, this wasn't the way I wanted to crack it open. Maybe being my own boss was something I worked on behind a full-time job, that way I was still making the bucks and yet funding myself and getting the clients so I wouldn't have such a shift from one job to my own. There was merit in it. Some.

With the fork in her hand, she circled my face. "That's what I like to see. The ideas swimming in your head."

"Well, thank you for putting them there." But I laughed because it was an intriguing thought.

Could it be done? Did I want my own PR and marketing firm? I had ideas, namely for Carter's coffee shop, but was that what I honestly wanted?

Chapter Five

HAVING BRAIDED MY long, brown hair and donned a baseball cap, I hoped I was practically unrecognizable as I strolled into the Coffee Loft later that week. I even ordered something different and skipped the donut, although the smell was intoxicating my waistline would thank me for it.

Trying to look like a university student – I wasn't so far removed that I couldn't pull it off – I set up my laptop in the darkened corner and clicked away. An idea sprung to mind, one that had been festering for some time on an old project for a former client. They had rejected it because it wasn't what they were looking for.

Extenuating data, that's what I needed, but not in the way a business looked at it. I wanted the emotional pull. What brings a customer back over and over?

The personal interactions.

The atmosphere.

The pricing, although if a person felt appreciated and the place was cosy, the price could skew higher.

That's what I desperately needed if my idea was going to hatch, and that's what I watched for over the course of five days, miraculously not drawing attention to myself as I blended into the environment, hoping I looked like a regular in the small mountain town. Every day I visited, always at different times, and I took notes on the type of people who visited and timed their visits. I wasn't gathering the financial information, Carter would surely have that, but I was curious to see who the customers were, not how many.

There were couples who lingered over coffees, shared desserts, and endless smiles.

Girlfriends who gathered and indulged in laughter and sometimes tears.

There were singles, mostly young men, who took their orders to go.

Families with young children were a rarity, and if they stopped by, it was typically take-out and a paper cup drink for either the mom or dad – rarely both.

I took notes on the customers, adding their perceived moods to my ever-growing spreadsheet, and typed as frantically as I could.

It wasn't just the customers I watched; it was the staff I studied as well, although two shined above the others. Harry was the main one, working afternoons and early evenings, and although he did his job well, he wasn't bubbly and was fairly strait-laced and even-keeled.

Another employee, Nina, seemed the same age as Harry but was wildly more engaging with the customers and they fed off that. When she bounced around, customers seemed to buy another pastry or have another cup of coffee. She was also a bit of a wild card, singing as she cleaned the tables or dancing to whatever song was playing overhead.

Carter didn't have a huge staff and had a couple of non-descript part-timers, but he wasn't busy enough to warrant needing more.

As I was returning from the bathroom on my fifth day of visits, Carter was walking around. I hadn't seen him out over my last couple of incognito visits, and during most of my undercover operations his name hadn't even been whispered.

However, there he was walking toward me with a small tray, and a fresh cup of steaming coffee on top.

"Figured I'd interrupt whatever work is keeping you highly focused and drop off a complimentary cup of joe for you. It's a brew-tiful day, isn't it?" He set the mug down, but it was his forearm I was staring at.

What was the draw to a sleeve rolled up exposing a forearm? It was captivating in a way I couldn't explain.

"Hey, my eyes are up here," he said with a hearty laugh.

My embarrassed gaze roamed up his sleeve, over the open top button of his shirt where a gold necklace barely peeked out, and up over his full lips to his gorgeous eyes. Which were narrowed slightly, although his left brow was raised ever so in a slightly curious look.

He nosed toward my laptop. "What have you been working on?"

"A mini project, actually."

"And that's what's been bringing you here for a few hours each day?"

My jaw unhinged and fell open in the most unladylike way. Abruptly, I snapped it shut and rolled my bottom lip between my teeth. "You noticed?"

"It's my store, of course I'm going to notice." He tipped closer, a breathy hint of mint in the air. "By the way, I liked the outfit you had on earlier this week – that blue sweater. It looked great on you." A faint blush tinged the apples of his cheeks.

The royal blue cable-knit sweater I'd paired with black jeans and my leather boots was one of my all-time favourites, and I felt comfortable and confident while wearing it.

A warm, blossoming heat rolled up from my insides and spread like wildfire across my chest, flooding into my ears at a rapid pace. How sweet he'd noticed me? I hadn't seen him then or the day previous, so where had he been hiding?

Trying to control my breathing, I leaned back slightly to allow for a greater intake of air. "Thank you for noticing. If I came dressed like I was ready for a business meeting, it would've raised alarm bells. I was trying to blend in."

"You're born to shine, and you just walking into a place draws attention. You could never blend." His gaze fell to the mug of coffee, and my heart thumped loudly in response. "Believe me, people notice you."

It was said so sweetly, I blushed even harder, which I didn't think was possible. Had the area been dark, I would've lit it right up.

"Anyway." He removed the ring-stained mug, added it to his tray, and shoulder-checked toward the front of the store. "I'm sorry about our last interaction. The cup of coffee is for you, not as a peace offering, just as a because. It's just a regular brew, nothing fancy." He kicked the top of his runners over the hardwood floors. "Ah, jeez. It is a bit of a peace offering."

"Thank you." I took a sip while keeping my focus on Carter. He hadn't returned my focus and was shuffling on his feet. "It's just what I needed, thanks." I set it down and cleared my throat, ready to tackle the elephant in the room. "Last time you and I talked, you took off abruptly. What happened? Why'd you just leave me?"

A heavy sound filled the space between us, and he slipped onto the chair across from me.

The napkin under the mug called to him and he retrieved it, folding it along the sides and giving it half his attention. However, he still avoided my question.

I prodded but squared my shoulders. "Was it because I was crying?"

With that, his chocolatey-brown gaze jumped up to lock on me as it widened in surprise. "Never."

"Really?" I narrowed my eyes in judgement.

A long time ago, I'd learned the quickest – and most awkward way – to clear the area around me was to lose control of my emotions, and few people rarely stuck around when it happened. Once my dad passed away though, I just stopped crying in front of people, or even coming close. No one cared, or they blamed it on that time of the month while they muttered under their breath, and it wasn't worth the awkwardness always accompanying it.

"Why'd you leave me like that?"

The Adam's apple bobbed, and he stopped manoeuvring the napkin into whatever it was he was creating. A swan? "I didn't leave you. I had something I needed to attend to and when I came back, you were gone."

My chin tucked in as I leaned forward. "I waited over an hour for you to return."

"Harry said as much." The tone was even and calm, but there was also an edge to it I couldn't quite put my finger on.

I waited. I watched. I hoped.

He remained rigid and unyielding, blinking evenly as if my narrowed gaze was having zero effect on him like it used to. No further explanation rolled out of him, no apology either. The conversation was over.

"That's all I'm getting?"

Finally, he looked at me, after first staring hard and long at my computer, and then extinguished a hearty breath. "Having some luck with the job search?"

"Actually, no. But I am working on something. Can I be blunt?"

He straightened in his spot, squared his shoulders, and swallowed. "You always were."

Dang. Didn't think it would come back to bite me in the butt, and yet here it was, some dozen and a bit years later.

Before I could embarrass myself further, I put a hint of professionalism into my tone as I inhaled and began. "What's your PR plan? I overheard a customer go on and on about how the Coffee Loft doesn't run any kind of promotions, how it's always the same thing."

"But it works, right? We're turning a nice profit, I get to do what I love, and everyone's happy. Besides, it's not always the same thing, occasionally we do introduce new flavours of coffee and pastries." There was more than a hint of defensiveness in his voice. "Our customer's ratings and reviews give the store a –"

"A 4.87 out of 5. I've done my homework." I smiled and set my hand on top of his, hoping to diffuse the sudden tension, but it was more than that. I craved his touch, and man, did it feel nice. "Do you have a quick business minute? I know you're always busy, but I have an idea for you."

With a slight hesitation, he clasped his hands together and put on his most serious face. It was impassive and hard to look at.

"I promise my idea won't hurt, or even cost you much investment."

"Okay." He swallowed loud enough to hear. "I'm listening."

I laid it all out before him, going against my gut, and showed him the raw data I'd collected over the past several visits – it was a small sample size, but it gave me a strong indication of his customer base.

If he was impressed, he hid it well, but the same could be said if he was upset. He was impossible to read, and it was infuriating.

"I propose we – or you – have a fun campaign, and we can set it to conclude on Valentine's Day."

"That's a long way away, we're barely at

Halloween."

I nodded and a stray strand of hair fell out across my forehead. It was long enough for me to tuck it behind my ear, and the whole time I did it, Carter's gaze had followed.

"Valentine's is three and a half months away. Things like my idea take time to create, build and implement, and you can't pop up and plan the idea with only a few short weeks. I mean, you could, but why?" I clicked over to another tab, showing off the Love Notes idea that sprang to me on a drive home. There were some mock images I'd created which desperately reeked of a third-grader competence since my designer skills were a total bust. Regardless, I continued with my unrehearsed spiel. "What makes the Coffee Loft so endearing? What keeps customers coming back?"

"Our high quality, ethically sourced coffee, and locally made treats," said without feeling, like he had been preprogrammed to have the answer ready on the fly.

I looked long and hard into his eyes, daring him to show some expression, but it was all for naught. Clearly, I needed to approach this from a different direction. "Is that what your customers say?"

"My reviews speak for themselves." Another

matter-of-fact statement.

"Yes, they do, and they speak volumes, but not one mentioned the ethically sourced coffee and only two mentioned the locally produced treats." For good measure, I produced the long listing of reviews and pointed out the two in question. "But don't get me wrong. Those are admirable, but it's not the reason the customer keeps coming back."

A slight crease formed between his brows.

"I'm just trying to help you be bigger than you ever thought possible. What is your end goal with the Coffee Loft?"

He blew out a long, drawn-out breath. "I'm already part of a chain."

"No, I got that, and there are locations sporadically throughout the US, and two in Canada, both in Alberta, with your store being one of them. How do we make the Coffee Loft a must-stop location for locals and the tourists travelling through to the mountains?"

"With A+ customer service."

"Of course." I was hitting a wall. A massive brick wall.

This was not going the way I'd envisioned. Stupidly, I thought he'd embrace the idea and get so excited, he couldn't wait to get started.

"Cara, what you are proposing is great, but I need to be blunt *with you.*"

My heart constricted as he spoke with a deep and familiar tone often used by my bosses. I braced myself for his words since the pitch of his voice seemed to be on the same level as his stoic expression. Deep down, my breath turned cold.

He shook his head, and the word barely breathed out. "No."

Chapter Six

THE SINGLE WORD sliced through my dwindling mood, chopping it up into pieces and spitting back as something ugly and callous.

I slammed the lid shut on my laptop, pulling back slightly when I heard a crack, and stuffed my belongings into my bag. "Well, thank you for your time and for the coffee."

My focus flew to the till, to get over there as fast as my wobbly legs could carry me, pay my bill, and hightail it out of Ridge Heights. I'd been so foolish in my thinking; I thought the love note idea was the best one I'd created – something his customers would eat up. But I was wrong. Again. No wonder I wasn't making it in this business. Tory had been right, I did suck.

"Cara, wait. Let me explain." He gripped my arm and spun me around, pulling me close enough to narrow the distance between us to mere inches.

I stared at the chain around his neck, rather than concentrate on the sensation of his warm fingers wrapped around my wrist.

"There's nothing to explain. Your *no* left very little wiggle room." It wasn't supposed to be snarky, yet I couldn't control the way it sounded.

Ignoring my snide comment, he stepped even closer. I could breathe in his sweet, intoxicating coffee bean scent, which wasn't fair. It was like a sedative, and I wasn't ready to calm down. Far from it.

"Let me explain." There was a sharp edge to his voice I'd never heard before, and it commanded my full attention.

Swallowing, I steadied myself in his eyes. "Okay."

"Sit down." When I had perched myself on the edge of the seat, he lost the hardness and softened with a gentle head-shaking sigh. "All marketing plans must get approval from head office to make sure they are consistent with branding, imaging, and all that. As much as I love your idea, because I do think it's truly unique and you know your stuff, I'd need to run it up the flagpole, so to speak, and see if they'd be on board with it."

"Oh." I pushed back deeper into my chair and slumped. The flickered flames of anger hadn't fully extinguished. Not yet. "Oh, okay. Well, I suppose that makes a little sense. You could've led with that."

"Based on your reaction..." A weak smile floated across his face. "I'm inclined to agree with you."

I had nothing to counter his statement. Heart on my sleeve – my domain since the day I was born.

"I'm glad to see something hasn't changed with you." His smirk deepened, and with it, a different sense of calmness was blanketing me. How the world did that work?

A long, lingering sigh blew from my lungs, extinguishing the last of the anger. Staying this close to him was undoing my limited self-control. "I really should get going. I have a long drive home, and the night has already fallen."

Once again, I rose, this time with great effort, as if leaving was the last thing on my mind. I didn't want to go, but I also knew I shouldn't stay. Or couldn't.

"Have dinner with me."

"Okay." The word slipped out fast – too fast as my heart was clearly running the logic show – however the growing smile it created on his face was worth the quick response.

"Give me a few minutes to make sure Nina can close, and we'll be off." He walked cautiously back to the counter, checking over his shoulder and connecting with me. A hand went in the air, showing off two fingers before he disappeared down the hall.

There needed to be another word for okay, but it wasn't coming to me. Instead, I stole glimpses down the hall to see where he was in between digs through my wallet for the cash.

I had just paid my bill when he returned. "So, where are you taking me for dinner?"

"How much of Ridge Heights have you seen?"

"Main Street and this coffee shop, and, hmmm... That sums up my experience."

He shook his head and pulled his black and red toque over it. "You've barely seen anything. We're so much bigger than one main street."

"I gathered."

"C'mon, I'll give you a quick tour as we go."

We stepped out into the crisp air. Although it was October, winter was heavy in the air, and the town lights were reflecting off the low-hanging clouds. Main Street had a rather ethereal view, like a city in the fog, and yet, there was none – just a gentle orangish haze.

Down the steps to the sidewalk, I stopped at my car, thankful I'd managed a spot near the shop. After pushing aside my small portable toolbox, I popped my laptop bag into the frunk and gave it a close as I slipped on my gloves. "Where are we going?"

"I'll take you to the place with the best view of Ridge Heights."

"Ooh, colour me intrigued. You know I love a good sightseeing spot."

"I've never forgotten." He glanced down to my footwear. "Glad to see you're wearing something more practical than *pretty shoes*."

"Of course. Never sure how far I'll have to park and walk, especially in this weather, and I'm not really a huge fan of falling." I licked my lips and stared at him.

The arm closest to me twitched and the elbow came nearer to me and then abruptly pulled back, almost as if he was warring with offering it. However, I wasn't slipping in my solid footwear, and as comfortable as we seemed to be with each other, I honestly didn't think we were at the point of linking arms. To me, that seemed next level when offered before it was a necessity – like last time.

He tipped his head to the left and spun on his heel. "This way. A block up, then a turn on Mountain Lane, and uphill for a bit."

"For a bit?" I followed, this time, matching him step for step. Wearing boots with grip was a sensible idea.

"Do you remember that place we visited back before we started our first year of college? Where we climbed the hill to the lookout point and had a picnic?"

The night of our second kiss.

It was a beautiful grassy hill surrounded by trees, aside from the lookout opening. Once through the small forest, the downtown stretched out and the river snaked between the business towers. Naturally, the view was better at night because the buildings in the core were lit up.

I nodded. "Yeah, it was amazingly gorgeous."

"This view is sort of like that."

"Well, that's raising the bar mighty high, Mr. Cross." A gentle chuckle rolled out, and I stole a sideways peek to watch his face morph into an upturned smile.

"You'll see."

The end of the block was quickly approaching

as we passed the stores. It felt as if we were walking at a slight incline. We rounded the corner onto Mountain Lane and continued following it uphill. It was the type of road situated between two blocks of buildings a passerby could've mistaken for a back lane as opposed to a true road. Must be one of those hidden gems the travel sites boast about.

"We need to cross here."

There was no crosswalk, no crossing lights, just the empty asphalt. It didn't even look like there was a sidewalk on the other side.

"You're right, this does feel like that lookout spot we went to." It was kind of eerie how similar it was starting out. Open roads. Stairs to climb. Just the two of us.

"Between those trees." He pointed across the snowy road we were navigating over. "There's a huge set of stairs. We'll climb those, and we'll be closer to the restaurant. It beats taking the long and windy road all the way up."

"Going to make me work for my supper, eh?" I laughed. "This had better be worth it."

The uphill walk was already causing my heartbeat to accelerate, doing a flight of stairs was going to send it atmospheric. I hoped I wasn't sweaty and red-faced at the top.

We stopped at the base of the wooden stairs which rose into the fresh-smelling forest for as far as I could see, and under the glow of the streetlight at the top, the top was still a flight or two away.

At first, I was all gung-ho and climbed the stairs like a rock star, but by the time we got to the fourth platform, I was feeling more than a little winded but fought against the rapid and loud exhales my body needed. I knew I was out of shape, but I didn't need to highlight it with bright neon arrows.

"All good?" Carter asked. "We're almost there."

Thank the Lord, who I felt I was going to meet soon if we had to keep going. I needed to cut back on the daily donuts and calorie-laden drinks at his shop, although Carter wasn't having any issues. Maybe he did these stairs daily and it was no big deal. Had to admire the stamina though.

He stopped and turned, giving me a minute to catch my breath. "You can see the rooftop patio on my building."

We were high above Main Street, which curved around the bend off to my left, with the rest of the town awash in an amber glow and dots of golden orbs sprinkled along the roadways. To say it was enchanting was an understatement.

"Wait, what?" I spun and looked through the clearing of trees. "Where?"

Carter stepped down a couple of stairs to stand beside me and pointed to a set of buildings to the right, which meant we likely walked by them as we strolled down the block. Why hadn't he said anything at the time?

"It's the unit above Meeples & Magic."

"Say again?"

"The local board game store."

"You play there?" Once upon a time, he'd been quite the Catan and Ticket to Ride player.

"On occasion, I'll join the group for a D&D session or a game of Magic the Gathering."

Not sure why it surprised me to learn Carter was a bit of a nerd, although I found the new information charming as it added to his appeal. Gerry was not a nerd, not in the smallest of hints – he was along the lines of a jock, but I couldn't tell you what sport he was most interested in. Football, rugby, soccer; they all seemed the same to me.

"Have you lived there long?" I asked and resumed my stair climbing.

"I don't know, roughly three years?"

I hid a forced exhale of air under a laugh. "No

anniversary celebration?"

Carter had been the type of guy to celebrate *everything,* and not just birthdays or anniversaries; the day he got his car, the first time he asked me out, the first time we… kissed.

He ignored my question and carried on. "It's the perfect size, just a one-bedroom with a huge kitchen and living room, and it's literally a block from the back door of work."

"If you had a tunnel, you wouldn't even need to step outside."

"And where's the fun in that? I love being outside. The fresh air is so good, especially here in the mountains. I just walk everywhere. Ridge Heights isn't that big."

The end was in sight. A few more steps. With a push of energy and a spring in my steps, I made it to the top, breathless but grateful. However, there was no restaurant. Just a snow-covered road.

"It's… not… here?" My words fell like my enthusiasm.

"Through there."

I followed the length of his finger to the trees on the opposite side. More blasted stairs. By the time we got there, I was going to have lost all my cuteness and look like I'd just run fifty miles, which of course, I couldn't do.

"Great. Well, you'd better keep talking. That's more stairs than I anticipated."

"Trust me, it's worth it."

"Better be." I crossed the road and swore a blue streak inside my head. "So. Tell me all about Ridge Heights."

"What do you want to know?"

Why he wasn't out of breath like I was? All these stairs seemed effortless on his part. Pangs of jealousy flared in my gut. Amanda wouldn't suffer with this either, in fact, she'd tackle it like Rocky Balboa.

"Everything. Why'd you move here?"

"That's a great question, and I don't have an answer to share."

To share? That sounded like a story; a juicy, pull-back-the-layers kind of sharing. I wanted more information, but at the moment, my focus went to lifting each tired, shaky leg to the next stair and trying to be cool and collected, not half a breath from death.

"I looked at places in Red Deer, but nothing was within walking distance of everything I'd need, and I didn't like the feel of the place. On a whim, I researched nearby small towns, searching for everything I needed within a short bike ride or a long walk, and on the same day, by happenstance, saw a listing for a Coffee Loft expansion. Made some phone calls, secured a few things, and bought the building." His voice went from soothing to concerned.

Had he heard my latest gasp of air?

"You doing okay?"

Good grief, he had heard. Embarrassment pushed me onward, and suddenly a renewed energy took hold, launching me closer to the streetlight several steps away. "I'm fine."

"The rest they say is history."

History? Oh yeah, his decision to snap up a property, buy a business, and move here. "All on a whim?"

"Sometimes taking a leap, albeit the scariest leap ever, can have the biggest rewards. I've never regretted my decision, not even on the darkest of days." As if it was the most natural thing, he grabbed my hand and tugged me along. "You made it. Come see."

We stepped off the boardwalk and off to the right was a magnificent sight. A tall, two-story stone building built into the mountainside with more string lights than I could easily count dangled over the patio area. If I stretched out my ears hard enough, a faint melody danced across the cool mountain air. Even more, as I stared and took it all in, the fluffiest of snowflakes fluttered around, wrapping us in what would be described as a Hallmark moment.

It was stunning and magical. Still attached to Carter's hand, I turned around to take in the valley below with its sparkling lights and muted roadways, gasping at the beauty beneath my feet. It marvellously held my breath.

A whisper felt too harsh, but that was the only level my voice croaked out. "Oh my, wow. I love string lights. And the snowflakes. And the magnificent view. Wow. It's beyond perfect."

Wrapped in the moment, and without any hesitation on my part, I spun into the one who brought me here and planted a kiss on his lips.

Chapter Seven

CARTER PULLED BACK from the quick, yet exhilarating kiss, and for a breathless moment, I watched as the falling snowflakes got caught in his long, dark eyelashes and then dissolved. He stared wordlessly, his gaze jumping from my left eye to my right as his head tipped curiously. In a heartbeat, he wiped the melted puddles from the apples of my cheeks with his gloved hand.

As tender as he was, his face spoke volumes; the expressions swirled like a hurricane. From amusement, to hurt, to pity, and stirring back to plain old curiosity. I'd overstepped, big time, and I needed to back peddle and mighty fast.

"I'm sorry, I'm so sorry," I said abruptly and stepped back, stomping down whatever indecisive idea caused me to react the way I did. Being impulsive never worked to my advantage – not with work, not in life, and most certainly not with Carter Cross.

Head shaking, I repeated my apologies breaking our connection and walking over to the main entrance of the restaurant and slinking inside.

"For two please," I said before Carter could speak. After all those stairs, I was hungry and we were going to eat, even if an elephant was going to join us. "And upstairs if there's anything available."

"Of course, this way."

After a quick glance back to Carter, who still hadn't uttered a sound and remained stoic in stance and expression, I followed the hostess up a long flight of stairs and over to a table next to the window. She'd blessed us with a spot overlooking the fading lights in the valley.

"It's perfect, thank you."

As she grabbed a pitcher of ice water and two glasses, I shucked out of my coat and draped it over the third chair before I took my seat, which wasn't as comfortable as I'd expected when looking from the outside in, but it would suffice. I'd half expected wingback chairs and elegant tablecloths versus the wooden chairs with red padded seats and paper placemats to decorate our space. Looks were deceiving.

Carter removed his winter gear and slid into a spot across from me.

"It was really beautiful outside with the stone masonry and all that." I looked anywhere but at him.

The sudden wave of awkwardness pressed on me like a thousand-pound weight, and I was going to crack soon if I couldn't change it.

"They really could use an update in the interior though. Although…" Glancing around, I shrugged – if they were going for an aged appearance, they'd hit the nail on the head. It was a blast out of 1970's décor, aside from the paper placements. "Maybe that's the look they were going for."

The air was cool, and my mouth was drier than the desert, so I took a hearty gulp of the ice water from the amber-coloured tumbler on my right.

After clearing his throat, Carter finally spoke. "About what happened outside."

The elephant pulled up a chair and got comfortable.

I put my hand up to stop him. "I'm so sorry. I'm going through a lot of issues in my life, and for a moment, it all culminated in one brief second and I was overcome with emotion. And the fact that it was you I was sharing it with."

But I couldn't promise him it wouldn't happen again, because I wanted it to, but next time, I wanted to feel him kissing me with passion, not returning the kiss like an afterthought before he broke us apart.

In the center of the table, there was a battery-operated candle lacking sparkle and sizzle but for some reason, it captured and held my focus. I dared it to roar to life, but it had to have been soaking up the tension around the table. It flickered, shone a quick burst of bright light, and then faded out of existence.

"I'm sorry too."

My shoulders fell and my heart plummeted into my stomach with a sour splash.

"It's not that I don't want to, because man-oh-man, I've waited a long time to..." His voice fell, and I met his gaze. "To kiss you again." He unclasped his cool hands and covered mine. "But I think it's not the right time. For anything serious."

A light scoffing sound breezed out of me as I leaned back, taking my hands with me and undecided about where they needed to go, I dropped them into my lap. "Because I've just gotten out of a relationship?"

"Not at all. Because of me."

I nodded and crossed my legs, folding my arms over my chest. "Ah, the whole it's-not-you-it's-me syndrome. Got it."

"It's more than that, and I wish I could explain."

Shaking my head, I flagged a server over, who promptly stepped up to the table. "Can I have a glass of your house red, please? And pronto."

"Sure thing, and you, sir?"

"Water's fine." Carter folded the edges of his placemat, creasing the lines firmly with the tip of his fingernail.

Like a knife through the silence, my wine arrived, and I took a decent-sized taste. It was disgusting and dry, but all my fault for not having asked about it to begin with.

Carter matched me sip for sip until we had both finished half our drinks.

I'd been on many awkward first dates, but this was worse, likely because I knew Carter, or at least had once upon a time. We'd known the other inside out and backward, but here we were years later, and in this moment, we were all strange and uncomfortable. Had I held my emotions in check, we could've been enjoying this togetherness, instead of him polishing up his origami skills while I drank my wine fast enough to give me a healthy buzz.

I set my empty glass down and let the words fall out. "This is an amazing view. You were right, it is breathtaking up here."

"It is. The spring and fall are the best times as the sun sets at a decent hour. Since we're facing east, we don't get to see a gorgeous sunset, but it's neat to see the shadows stretch out across the town. It's quite the sight."

"Yeah, it's nice."

Oh geez, we'd been reduced to small talk, and that bothered me as it was similar to work conversations. No one bothered to get to know another person so if the talk wasn't work-related and there were no discussions about who was doing what on which file, it was conversations revolving around the weather. Pathetic. I was better than that, and so was Carter.

Had my kiss spoiled everything building between us? Dang.

Shifting the topic into one I knew he'd enjoy, I took a sip of my water, and then dunked the tip of my finger in so I could run it over the top of my glass.

"How's your family? What have they been up to lately?"

My questions broke his concentration, and he looked up from deepening the creases on his placemat. He was creating a frog. "They're good. Darcy has a daughter and is married to Stark—"

"Stark?" I raised a brow.

"Legally, it's Starkland, but he goes by Stark."

"That's… well, that's highly unusual. What did they call their daughter?"

"You'll love this." A weak smile teased his lips, and I waited on bated breath. "Starcy."

I covered my mouth and fake coughed to cover the laugh. There was no way he was serious, except he was.

He shook his head. "She'll be teased all her life. We all begged Darcy to give it some thought but she believes it's the perfect mashup of her and her husband's name. I call her my little star, so that helps."

"That's sweet."

Darcy was barely a year younger than Carter and was flighty, impulsive, and a true wild child; the kind who threw caution to the wind and hoped for the best. Lady luck had often been on her side as everything ended up working in her favour.

"And what's she doing now?"

"Starkland inherited something in the ballpark of a bazillion dollars, and they are overseas somewhere blowing it faster than humanly possible." There was a strong hint of anger and disgust in his tone, and he huffed on the last word.

Being a mother wasn't a word I'd associate with Darcy, but his description sounded like the sister I remembered. "And Alison and Beatrice?" The older two sisters were already in university when Carter and I started dating. "What are they up to?"

"Alison is living her best life. She's running a pre-loved bookstore in the heart of downtown Calgary. Single and childless with plans on staying that way forever. Was married for eleven months but had the most awful of divorces."

"Oh, that bites."

Alison had always been the nicer of the two older sisters. She was warm and comforting, the quintessential big sister who doted on me and treated me like I was blood family, and not her brother's girlfriend. We had fun together. However, when Carter and I went our separate ways, we'd fallen away as well – loyalty to her brother and all that.

The oldest sister was tough as nails and told me many times if I ever hurt Carter, she'd make it so my body would never be discovered. She scared me. A lot.

I cringed before I asked. "And Bea?"

He dropped his gaze to the table and resumed his paper creasing. He twisted in his seat and pinched the bridge above his nose. "About her." A sharp inhale of air preceded a swig of water. "I need to be honest with you."

A ribbon of morbid curiosity coursed through my veins, and I'd worried something awful had happened. I braced for the worst case while I ran through thoughts and ideas of what could cause Carter to look so concerned. "Is she okay?"

With that, he locked onto my eyes and held firm for a heartbeat. "She's fine. Actually, she's better than fine." He fiddled with the edges of his placemat.

"Why the cloak and dagger?" He was hiding something, but it was hard to figure out how bad it was. He claimed she was okay, so the way his words and demeanour changed sent up a few red flags.

"There's no... well... I haven't been honest with you."

My sigh was forced out in a quick whoosh.

Another flag shot up.

"You see, the thing is, Beatrice, well she, and I'm not." His expression swirled and changed with each broken sentence. It was impossible to stay on any one thought for more than a microsecond. "Geez, Louise." He stopped his fiddling and clasped his hands together firmly, his knuckles turning white. "Listen, I'm not the big shot you think I am. I'm a fraud."

My eyes narrowed in confusion. In fact, my brow pushed so low over my right eye, it was almost like an awning over a shop window. "I'm not really following you."

"Bea owns the Coffee Loft." His shoulders fell and rolled forward with the admission. "I own the building, but she has the rights to the franchise. In essence, I work for her. I'm the manager, but not the owner."

"Oh." I sat up straighter and let the words sink in. That wasn't at all bad. "What's wrong with that?"

"I was trying to impress you. To show you I've done big things with my life." Crimson was splashing out from behind his beard, up over his cheeks, and heading straight into his hairline.

"Oh, Carter. You don't have to worry about

impressing me."

"Yeah, I do. When I left you to go overseas to study, I planned to come home and be this big shot. Someone you deserved. Someone who would lavish expensive gifts on you and whisk you away on last-minute tropical vacations. We'd bring our three kids and we'd see the world, like Darcy is doing."

I reached out to hold his hand. "You envisioned us with three kids?"

"Yeah. Two boys and a little sister they doted on."

My heart skipped a beat, and my breath caught in my chest. As much as I had hoped, I never knew he had envisioned such a future for us. "That's probably the sweetest thing I've ever heard."

"You need to get out more." The blush faded as he grew some strength.

"Yeah, well, the jury is still out on that one." Still, I had questions. Lots of them. "So, if you had all these big plans for us, why did the communication drop? Why did you decide to end us?" The first of two devastating moments in my life; the kind deep down I'd never gotten over.

Once again, his focus fell, just like his rolled in shoulders. "Because I came to the realisation how, even though you deserved all those things and so much more, some things in my life had changed to the point where I knew I was never going to be able to give them to you."

"Like what?" What could he have possibly done that would've affected us? Had he kicked a puppy or something? Because that was a deal breaker for sure, although I couldn't imagine Carter could even think such a thing.

"Just… things. We can never be more than just friends."

My brows pinched together, and not caring about my makeup, I rubbed my hands over my face in a weak effort to wipe away the questioning yet witchy face I knew was settling over me. It was a bad reaction and all it did, as my former boss would say, is to turn people off. "Well, that's not much of an explanation."

"I know. I'm sorry, but it's all I can give. I wanted to give you the world, but it turned out, I couldn't even give you all of me. I can't. I'm not worth it. I'm not the man you deserve, so I set you free. I had to." Like he'd just been shocked, he jumped out of his seat, shrugging, and muttering under his breath. "I'm so sorry, Cara, but this isn't fair to you."

In a heartbeat, Carter zipped down the stairs.

Fishing around in my purse, I located some change and piled it up, making sure I had enough to cover my wine and a small tip. By the time I got outside, Carter had vanished into thin air. No footprints in the freshly fallen snow. Nothing. What was going on with him?

Chapter Eight

UNIMPRESSED WITH CARTER'S abrupt departure, I descended back into the town, angrier than I had been when he rejected my marketing idea. Thankfully the trek down the stairs was easier, although my knees were threatening to lock up.

I wanted answers and Carter had them all.

Why was he *not worth it*? Who had told him that lie? But most importantly, I wanted – needed – to know what happened between the third year of college and a few years ago. He was hiding something, I just had to figure out what and uncover it.

Wandering down Main Street, I stomped past several stores – two of which had for sale signs posted in the windows and another had a help wanted sign. Another advertised an upcoming Christmas workshop making Grinch Trees which sounded like fun. Mentally, I added it to my calendar until I stopped outside the Meeples & Magic game store, sending my focus up the brick building to the level above where a light shone through the patio window. Was that his place? Or the darkened room beside it?

Did I dare knock or buzz, assuming I could locate the door? The lone door on the front had a closed sign hanging underneath their logo, and there was no way I was walking through a darkened alleyway to locate a back door.

Rather than do anything productive, I paced back and forth, wearing out a path through the fluffy snow in front of the store, with a baited hope Carter would come to the window, see me, come to his senses, and rush right down to talk and work things out.

He had to know I was here for him. Whatever it was, I would understand.

Nothing of the sort happened because I just wasn't lucky like that.

Discouraged, defeated, and needing to defrost, I sulked down the street and hopped into my car, checking a couple of times to make sure he hadn't magically appeared, called my name, and somehow I'd missed it in the process.

I needed to stop watching romantic movies – life just wasn't like that.

In typical Cara fashion, my emotions got in the way and ruined what could've been a good thing. I really needed to learn to keep them from exploding out.

TWO DAYS LATER, after a semi-successful Pilates session in my living room, Amanda and I sat around my table, drinking bottled coconut water she claimed would help flush the fat out of my system. I wasn't so convinced.

"Any luck on the job front?" Amanda asked after downing her bottle and ending with an *ahh*.

"Nothing. There hasn't been anything I've gotten excited about. Except..." I trailed off and left the word hanging in the air like a pinata.

Amanda aimed her stick and took aim. "Except, what?"

I twisted in my seat and wiggled my shoulders. "I don't understand it myself, but there was this workshop in Ridge Heights where they are making Grinch trees."

"What in tarnation are those?"

"Cedar trees wrapped in wire to bend them, so they are hanging over their pot. They are then wrapped in ribbon and have an ornament hanging from the tip."

She screwed up her face. "Lame."

"No way. They're really cool. My dad used to order a couple for his shop for decorations. They're quite neat." I flipped through my phone until I found a couple to show Amanda.

She stared, unconvincing, while scratching the side of her lip. "Meh. They're okay."

"I think they're neat." Resigned, I set my phone down.

"What does that have to do with the job front?"

It was a wild idea, but the fact remained, aside from Carter, I hadn't thought about much else. "I'm not sure. There was a help wanted sign in the window and—"

"And you're going to apply? For a menial seasonal job in a small town? Cara, I'm sure you can find cedar bending activities here if that's what you're willing to do."

I was ticked off by the tone of her voice. "Menial?"

"You didn't attend four years of university to

bend cedar trees. Come on."

"I know that."

"And you don't live in Ridge Heights."

"Again, something I know." Not sure why I thought she'd be excited about the idea. It was a job, something I was semi-enthused about, which was more exhilarating than anything in recent weeks.

"What's your fascination with that place? Still hooked on the ex-boyfriend?"

I rose and went into the kitchen, staring into the fridge until I found the carton of coffee creamer I wanted. Pouring a splash into my cup, I added in the full amount of fresh coffee and readied a straight black coffee for my friend.

"I kissed him." I set the mugs down with zest. Coffee splashed over and ran down the sides.

"You dawg." Those two words were dragged out for several seconds as she craned a perfectly manicured eyebrow into her bangs.

I slumped into my seat opposite her. "But there was nothing on the other side of the kiss to suggest there could ever be more. In fact, he seemed almost weirded out about it all."

"That's bizarre."

"And he went on saying how we could never be anything more than friends."

"Why's that?"

I lifted my shoulders to practically touch my ears and let them fall with a solid release. "I have no idea. Maybe he talked to Gerry and decided I wasn't worth it."

"Stop it."

"It's true. Gerry thought I wasn't girlfriend material as I didn't seem to remember things about him and who knows, maybe Carter knows him, and they've been talking."

"Do you know how unlikely that scenario is?"

"Then why would he say that?" A sting of rejection stabbed my words. "I kissed him, and he didn't kiss me back."

She placed her warm hand on me. "I don't know. Maybe he's got lots of heartache and trauma from past relationships and he's treading carefully?"

It was a valid thought, and it did make some sense. He *had* mentioned an ex-girlfriend who had done something to him, but he hadn't expanded on what the *something* was.

"You're so into him, aren't you?"

"Once upon a time, he held my heart." There was no hesitation and my words slipped out as easy as breathing.

She scooted her chair over to me and stared into my soul. "Tell me about Carter. You've never mentioned him until recently. Before that, I didn't even know someone had the pleasure of truly holding your heart. That, my friend, is a rare gift."

My heart smiled. "Back in high school, I had the biggest crush on him. All the girls did. He was smart, funny, shy, and so dreamy. We'd been friends in drama class and often just hung out, but that's all I was, the tag along."

"Wait a hot minute? You were a drama chick?"

A weak grin snuck out. "Yeah, and I totally sucked. In fact, I almost failed the class."

"How is that possible? Don't you get points just for showing up?"

I waved a hand through the air. "It doesn't matter. Can I explain about Carter?"

"Yes, yes. Go on." She blew across the top of her mug and took a quick sip.

"Then I took the bold step of asking him out. It was just to the coffee shop around the corner from school."

"Wait, you went out for coffee on your first date?" She tipped herself forward.

"Yeah. What's the big deal?" Going to the movies was so cliché, and this way, if things hadn't gone well, he had an easy out to leave. A coffee wasn't a huge time commitment.

"And he now owns a coffee shop? Hmm."

It was a coincidence, but still. "You're making a huge leap."

"Am I?"

"But he doesn't own the coffee shop, just the building."

"I thought you said he did."

"I thought so too, but would you let me finish?" I flashed back in time, recalling every detail as if it were on a screen in front of me. "On our first date, he wore black jeans, high tops, and an emerald-green sweater that somehow enhanced his dark brown eyes. He brought me a gift too."

"A single stemmed rose?" She pitched forward even more, and her voice softened to a barely audible level.

"Nah, that had never been his style. It was a mug."

Amanda scoffed and flung herself back into her seat. "A mug?"

"Yeah."

I hopped out of my chair and dug through my cabinet. Even after all these years, I still had it. Pulling it from the back, I turned on the hot water.

She joined me in the kitchen. "That grey mug, for real?"

"He remembered me saying how much I enjoyed the Phantom of the Opera. I loved the music and never got a chance to see it live. Then one day, he was out walking through the thrift stores, and he saw this." I held up the silver, glittery mug with one hand and ran my finger under the tap. The heat burned.

"Okay, big deal. It says The Phantom of the Opera on it. Two points to him for getting you a used coffee cup."

"It was brand new in the box and it does this."

I filled the mug and set it on the counter, willing it to work like it used to. Surprisingly, it did exactly what it needed to. It started changing. A white mask almost floated into existence and the image became sharper.

Her eyes grew larger. "Wow. That's cool."

"Right?" I dumped out the water and set the mug upside down on the dry rack. It was going to go back into its spot when it was dry. Out of fear of something happening to it, I never used it. "He said he found it the afternoon I asked him out."

She headed back to the table. "I'm still in shock you asked a guy out."

"I wasn't going to wait for him." It was true. Sure, it was scary as all get out to have asked him, but that sweet *sure* he gave me for an answer was totally worth it. "And over hot chocolates, he said he was relieved I'd asked him out as he'd wanted to ask me out but wasn't sure how. He was grateful I took that fateful first step."

"And afterward, you just became a couple?"

"Mostly. It took a bit of time. We didn't have our first kiss until a couple of weeks after the coffee shop date."

"Aww." She folded her hands together and rested her chin on them.

"Once we started university, we were inseparable, and as awful and cliché as it sounds, we were two pieces of a puzzle. Then, at the end of our second year, he got an amazing scholarship offer which took him overseas and kept us apart. At first, it was only to be for the first semester, but then it got extended. I was expecting to see him over the Christmas break, but he had a job there and couldn't leave. It was one thing after another, and the long distance was just too hard. In the end, he said it was over. I graduated alone." I took a drink and stared at Amanda, waiting for her to say something.

Instead, a calm yet pensive look filled her face.

"I'm curious. What did Gerry wear on your first date, and where did you go?"

Narrowing my eyes, I tipped my head to the side like a dog does when asked a bizarre question. "What does that have to do with anything?"

"Just answer the question."

I blinked and shook my head, doing my best to remember. "We went to a Baker-Bloom work function."

"And he wore?"

"I don't know, a black suit?" It wasn't important.

"You're guessing."

My head bounced around like a bobblehead toy. "What does it matter?"

"Because without any prompting, you recalled what Carter wore and where you went, but you struggled with Gerry. You probably even remember how he smelled."

Like body wash; clean and fresh.

"Yeah, so." But I saw where she was going with her inquisition. "First loves are different. They sit on a pedestal in the long list of broken heart moments."

"Yes, they are special, and yes, they are put on a pedestal." She sighed and shook her head. "I can't believe I'm going to say this, because I'm not a big pusher of happy ever afters and fairy tales, but dang." She sighed again. "You need to go to him. Take the temporary job at that tree-bending place and make all the weird ornaments your little heart desires. Get to know the guy again. Make him fall in love with you once more."

"I can't do that. He doesn't want to."

"He does, but clearly, there's something preventing him from taking that step. Just like when you asked him out."

I reflected on our conversation, and he had said he'd wanted to, but he couldn't. Did I need to push him? It wasn't what I wanted. I wanted to be sought after, to feel important enough that the guy wanted to make the first move. For once, just one time, I wanted to be chased.

However, it's hard to be chased when we're not even in the same area.

"So you think I need to move there and take the menial job?"

"Honestly, yeah." Her head bobbed a resounding yes. "Take a couple of months, work in a retail job with customers, not clients, and get to know Carter again. Who knows? Maybe the change will be good for you, and you'll come back here, clear-headed, and ready to move on. And maybe, just maybe, you'll bring Carter back with you."

"For real? You think I should?"

"I think you'd better. Should I help you pack?"

Chapter Nine

PACKING UP AND moving wasn't as simple as I expected or hoped. First, I needed a place to go, and there weren't too many available options in Ridge Heights, however, as a last resort there was a motel in town that rented rooms by the week and month. It wasn't fancy, but thankfully it was clean and came with a tiny, yet workable kitchenette. Ironically, given the age of the place, it had the type of charger I needed for my car Casper. I told the owner I'd take the place for a couple of weeks and paid in full.

By the middle of November with a quick wave and a tear-free goodbye from Amanda, who had lovingly helped me pack, I drove to the mountainside town with a full car. I kept my apartment in the city as a fallback for when this whole blasted idea fell apart and had brought with me the things I thought I'd truly need; the Phantom mug being one of them.

Once settled, as much as one could in a tiny 200 square foot space, and after a night of tossing and turning, I ventured out for a long morning walk, strolling the long length of Main Street until I stopped outside Daisy & Dahlia.

Steeling myself, I pushed down a morsel of fear and stepped inside, taking the help wanted sign off the window by the door and walking to the counter. Along the way, I removed my jacket and folded it over my arm.

The place smelled amazing with the mixture of fresh flowers permeating the air and it was like walking through a field, instantly whisking me back to childhood memories of rolling down a long grassy hill and stopping to sniff the wildflowers along the way.

The man behind the counter set down what he was working on and watched me approach, looking at me over his glasses. "Can I help you, miss?"

"I'm new in town and saw your sign." I set it on the counter, along with my jacket. "I have open availability and can work anytime. Your Grinch Tree workshop caught my attention, and I just happen to love those trees. We had them all the time when I was younger." I pushed my shoulders down as I looked up at the giant.

He was tall, broad-shouldered with a weathered face you just knew by looking at him how he didn't accept nonsense from anyone.

"Ever worked in a flower shop before?" His raked gaze sized me up.

"Never. But I'm a quick study and work well under minimal supervision." Besides, how hard could it be?

"I see. Do you happen to have a resume or something I can look at? Contacts? References? I can't just hire you all willy-nilly." He shifted on his feet, but his stance never changed.

However, my composure was falling and fast. "To be honest, Sir, I'm probably the last person you should hire."

His expression fell, as it should've, causing him to lean forward on the counter with rapt interest. "Oh? Why's that?"

"You see, Stanley," as I read his nametag. "I have a background in marketing, not in floral arrangement, but I'm going through a few things in my personal life causing me to leave my city life behind, move here, and start fresh. Maybe it's the clean, crisp mountain air, but there's something about this town that's calling out to me." He didn't need to know it was a guy because that sounded pure crazy.

There was no reason for him to think I was some lusty man-chaser taking a job just to knock the socks off the man I was desperate to reconnect with.

With a hopefully subtle shake of the head, I carried on. "However, for the first time in a long time, I'm listening to my gut. It told me I needed to be here, to switch fields and try this out. I'm likely to stumble and fall many times over, but I'm not a quitter, and you'll soon see that. In fact, even when things aren't working out, I tend to be loyal beyond reason. If you hire me, I will try my very best to be an outstanding employee."

"A background in marketing you say?"

"Yes, Sir." I hoped he heard beyond that because it was Grade-A verbiage, and I had impressed myself.

Standing back up to his full height, he rubbed his grey stubbled chin. "Hard worker too?"

"Of course. Without complaints."

"Alright. You've garnered my attention. What's your name, Miss?"

"Cara." I extended a hand. "Cara Gallagher."

He gripped it and squeezed, but not in the death grip way in which I'd become accustomed to over the years from the bigwigs. He wasn't trying to dominate me, and I appreciated that.

"Well, Cara Gallagher, I like your gumption, and I do believe everyone should have a second chance in life." He broke the handshake and dipped below the counter, producing a piece of paper and pen. "Tell you what I'll do. I'll hire you until the end of December, but after that, well, that'll depend on you, Miss."

That gave me five weeks to get things figured out. Totally workable.

"Thank you, Sir." I wished I could add a *you won't be disappointed,* but it wouldn't be the truth, and I was desperately trying to start on the right foot.

"Can you start tonight? I have a full workshop and there's just me hosting. I'd be grateful for an extra set of hands." He scribbled across the paper, but I was unable to discern what he'd written.

"I'd be honoured."

He dropped the pen onto the counter. "Fabulous. Workshop starts at six-thirty in the space next door, but I'll need you here by four, to help bring over the mini trees and all the materials." He eyed me up and down. "And as professional as I run my business, do you have anything else to wear?"

I gazed down at my black linen pants and white blouse. Perhaps I had overdressed, but I wasn't sure how to answer.

"Jeans are acceptable, as is a thicker sweater. You could ruin your nice shirt working here and it can sometimes be a little chilly as there's a draft in the space next door. Wear a decent pair of runners or work boots, do you have those?"

"I brought a pair of sneakers."

"Excellent, wear those since you'll be on your feet all night. I'll provide you with an apron and gloves and the coffee's always on. Sound fair?"

"Exceptionally." I extended my hand once again. "Thank you. I'll be here at four o'clock sharp, Sir."

He nodded. "Just call me Stanley, please."

"I will. Next time. Thank you."

"Alright. See you at four."

With that, I grabbed my jacket and pulled it on before I stepped out, took a few steps toward the vacant building where I hoped Stanley couldn't see me, and air-punched a dancing snowflake..

There was a spring in my steps as I headed deeper along Main Street toward my favourite coffee shop, but first I needed to call Amanda and share the good news.

My call went straight to voice mail – she must've been in court. Dang.

I ascended the steps into the Coffee Loft and beelined straight to the counter, ready to spend part of my first Ridge Heights paycheck before I'd even worked the hours to earn it.

Scanning the boards, there was a new flavour of donuts, and despite the scream from my waistline, I just had to try it.

"Let's change things up a little. One lofty-sized Maple Macchiato and a maple cream dipper, please. In the Snoopy mug please." I pointed to the eggshell blue mug with Snoopy on his back atop his doghouse.

"Sure thing," Nina sang out. "Give me a cuppa," she tossed a wink in my direction, "and I'll bring that over to ya."

"Thanks."

Turning, I headed to my favourite spot, but I stopped in my tracks when I saw Beatrice and Carter talking in hushed tones down the hallway. It was definitely Beatrice with her short blond pixie cut which brought out her high cheekbones, and a sense of class radiated out of her. Based on her appearance alone, she would've fit in perfectly as one of the senior partners of Baker-Bloom. She almost looked out of place in a coffee shop.

Tucking my chin down, hoping neither spotted me, especially her, I scoured the place to find a seat to keep me out of sight. Carter, I was okay with seeing again, but not his sister.

Slinking my way to the darkened corner, instead of taking the seat with the view, I faced into the corner but it rubbed me the wrong way as I had my back to the place. Warring against seeing the people and being exposed versus cowering, I chose the first option and swung over where I was visible but had the better view. I tipped my head down, covered my face with my left hand, and typed out a quick message to Amanda.

Didn't have the greatest sleep, but I got the job. Now, onto plan whatever comes next.

It would be some time before she got back to me, so I flipped over to my social media pages and scrolled. Nothing caught my attention. I looked up Daisy & Dahlia and scanned their page. It was lackluster with a few dozen posts, if that, and only one mentioned the workshop.

My mind started reeling with ideas and possibilities, but before I let it spiral out of control,

I closed out of the app and put my phone face down. Stanley didn't hire me for marketing, he hired me for workshop assistance. That had to be my focus.

Nina danced her way over, tray held high in her left arm, and stopped at my table.

I gave her my best smile. "Hey, is there a library in town?"

"Of course. You'll find it nearer the highway on Palisade Drive. It's beside the hospital, I think." It sounded like neither was a place she frequently visited.

"Thanks."

"You were here a lot not too long ago, and then you stopped. You new in town or something?" She tucked the tray under her arm exposing a tattoo on the underside before it was hidden from view.

I centered the donut in front of me and pushed the mug off to the side. "Just moved here."

No need to elaborate on how *just* that was.

"Figured as much. Welcome. Where ya 'riginally from?"

"Red Deer."

"Hole in the wall, that place is." She shook her head, and I swore the colours in it almost seemed to shimmer and change. "I couldn't wait to escape the madness. What a bunch of po-dunks."

"It's not that bad."

And it wasn't. I liked how centrally located it was. One hundred and three minutes north and I was in the capital city. Ninety-six minutes south and I was in the heart of Calgary. Plus, the mountains were less than two hours west of Red Deer. What wasn't to love?

"The job market isn't hot right now, 'specially here, so here's hoping ya can telecommute? But the people, like, they're really great and friendly. That's the reason I hang around."

"Thanks. I look forward to meeting more locals."

"You ought to come to the Tree Lighting ceremony on December 1. The whole dang town shuts down, aside from a few specific places, and we all gather at the town square. It's nifty. Tree lighting. Figure skating. All the hot cocoa you can drink. Truly, y'all, it's the best way to kick off the holidays." She was practically jumping from foot to foot.

Carter re-entered the shop and stomped his feet by the door – I hadn't even noticed he'd left. Scanning the place, he locked eyes with me, gave me a friendly wave, and disappeared down the hall. Dang, he looked first-rate as always, like he'd just stepped away from a photo shoot.

I tried giving my attention back to Nina. "When's that, the tree burning thing?"

"Tree *lighting*, and it's on the first." She wiggled while standing on the spot while I mentally face-palmed myself because when she said it, it hit me how she already *had* said when it was. And I was paying attention until Carter entered. "I think like around seven or something? I can look it up for you, if you'd like."

"Oh no, I won't trouble you. I'm sure I can search it out."

If the whole town shut down, surely there'd be signs. Maybe my new boss would have information on it as well.

"It's great. You'll love it. I met my true love there under the stars two years ago."

"That's sweet."

With the words hanging in the air, she read the space correctly and spun on her heels. Ten points to her. "If there's anything else I can grab for ya, holler, mkay?"

"Will do."

A few minutes after she'd left, I crashed in the wake of her sugar rush. Nina was a sweetheart. An effervescent soul. The world needed more of her.

Flipping open my favourite reading app, I scrolled through until I landed on my favourite Katie O'Connor novel. It was a comfort read, and one I'd read at least three times over the past year. I was just getting to the juicy part when a voice greeted me.

"To what do I owe this brew-tiful surprise?"

Despite the fact I wanted to see him, I just couldn't control the words shooting out of my mouth. I cocked an eyebrow, ignoring his pun. "Well, well, well. If it isn't the disappearing man."

"Says the one who hasn't graced my doorway in a couple of weeks."

"You ran first."

"Yeah. It's a problem, I know." When his gaze fell, his hand went up and gave the back of his neck a solid rub, or maybe a squeeze because his face flooded with a rush of colour.

"Why is that? That's twice now you've left me in a lurch." I held two fingers to punctuate my statement.

Those dark eyes narrowed into sad, narrow slits. "You wouldn't understand."

"Actually, I think I would." I rested my chin into the palm of my hand and gazed up at him, trying an old tactic that used to get me everything I wanted from him back in the day. "We used to share a lot."

"Things change."

My voice fell and softened. "Carter, whatever it is that's causing you to dash out every time I open up to you, I'm pretty sure I can handle it. If it's me, and something I'm doing, please just tell me."

"It's not you." He turned his head, stopping to stare toward the back hall before he focused on my donut. "Good choice. It's our new flavour."

"Thanks, but you're deflecting."

A tight fist formed at the end of his arm, making his sinewy muscles pop. "It's complicated, and this isn't the place."

Of course, he was correct. Whatever it was holding him back, it was obviously personal, and telling me in his workplace was not ideal.

"Fine. But soon, okay?"

"Okay." The locked expression promised me a story, and I for one couldn't wait. "Maybe."

In the meantime, I had to put my plan into motion. After all, he was the reason I had jumped ship and swam in his direction.

"So, the other day, I was doing some clean up, and guess what I found?"

He ran his fingers through his thick blond hair

and sighed, although a small smile was spreading across his lips.

"That Phantom mug you gave me on our first date."

His eyes grew wide, and the smile stretched into a full-blown grin. "Oh my word, you still have that?"

"I do. And, it still works."

"That's amazing." He took a seat across from me and lowered his voice. "I need to find another like it to display on the Mug Wall."

Quickly, I tossed my gaze over to the display. It would make a neat addition, but there was no way I was giving it up.

"Actually, I found a lot of things while cleaning this week." It had been eye-opening and my heart squeezed with all the memories flooding back when I found the old pencil box of keepsakes.

"Like?"

"Movie tickets. Concert tickets. That rock."

He nodded along and stopped suddenly. "Wait, what rock?"

"Remember the night when you got the flat on the highway, and the two of us in the pouring rain changed the tire?"

His sweet laugh wrapped around me. "I'd

forgotten about that. What a night."

"Right? All the thunder and lightning circling us, and somehow, we managed our first-ever tire change."

"We were soaked to the bone."

"And muddy because we had to make sure the jack was positioned correctly."

"That's right." He nodded.

"After we put the stuff back into the trunk, there was this heart-shaped rock. It wasn't very big." I demonstrated by cupping my palm. "But I kept it. Like a memento."

A dreamy look mellowed his features, and the crease on the edge of his eyes pushed higher. "We had a lot of fun, didn't we?"

"We sure did." My heart swelled recalling all the memories we made. Some hard, some sad, but overwhelmingly, the great ones won out. "And all because I asked you out."

"If you hadn't... I don't know if I would've ever had even the courage to try."

"Sure you would've."

He shook his head. "No way. You were this incredible breath of fresh air. Personable, you got along with everyone, and I mean everyone; staff, students, it didn't matter. You were smart, but not nerdy. You were well-known but not popular. You were gorgeous but…"

"But?" Desperate to hear the rest of his statement, I turned my left ear in his direction.

"There's no but. You were the best-looking girl in the whole dang school."

A wave of embarrassment washed over me, but it was mixed with a sense of pride. Aside from my father, no one since Carter had ever mentioned how I was beautiful, and here he was years later, saying it again.

"And *you* asked *me* out. All your life, you'll never know what that felt like."

I grimaced and pulled back a little, waiting for a response.

"I mean, the sweetest girl ever asked out the low-level drama kid. It's like a dream come true. Life doesn't get much better than that."

"Sure it does. You asked me out on the second date."

There was a hint of a sparkle twinkling in his eyes, the kind that sent my butterflies soaring. "You mean *hey, that was fun. Let's do it again?*"

And just as quickly, it faded away. However, my way in had been established.

I cleared my throat. "In keeping with our

tradition, I hear there is this amazing tree lighting ceremony going on this weekend."

He perked up once again.

"And I was wondering how I get a guy like you to take a girl like me to see this event in person."

The Adam's apple bobbed in his throat, but as I watched, a new expression replaced the self-deprecated look. "Well, I guess, you could ask. Or I could? But I'm not very good at this kind of thing."

"Try me."

He cleared his throat. It took a few solid seconds, but he finally blurted out breathlessly, "Do you want to go to the tree lighting ceremony with me on Saturday?"

Being the silly I was, I tapped my chin pensively. "Hmm… I'll have to check my calendar. Saturday, you say?"

His jaw dropped and his eyes widened, but then it must've hit him who he was dealing with as a large laugh roared out of him.

"Yeah, I'm free, and I'd love to join you. Thanks for asking."

That made his smile grow even larger, which I didn't think was possible. He rose and stood, wiping away an imaginary crumb as I hadn't even had a chance to taste the new donut yet.

"So, Saturday... I used to be the kind of guy who would pick up a girl and drive her around but with you... well, not living here, would it be possible..."

His sudden awkwardness was so cute, it was charming.

"Would you mind parking at my place, and we can walk over together? It would help me feel more manly about the whole situation."

"I wouldn't mind at all."

His shoulders sagged with relief. "Whew. Great. Thanks. See you Saturday around six? The actual tree ceremony is around eight, but you'll want to check out the food trucks and other fun festivities before that."

"I'll be outside your place by six."

"Dress warm too. There are firepits, but you'll want to keep your toes from freezing."

"I promise I'll dress for the weather."

"Great." He flipped his gaze back to the counter. "I should get back to work as I've been doing enough pro-caffeinating."

A gentle laugh breezed out with his words. The guy was funny, and on point with his puns.

"See you Saturday."

"Who knows, you may see me before." I

winked.

With a slight spring in his steps, he moved toward Nina and talked about whatever they normally discussed.

I, on the other hand, sent a quick text message to Amanda.

I got him to ask me out. Step one is in motion.

Chapter Ten

HOURS LATER, DRESSED in jeans and an old sweatshirt from my alma mater, I entered Daisy & Dahlia's five minutes early feeling out of place yet eager to start something new.

"Evening, Miss." Stanley set a box on the counter and looked me up and down over the tops of his glasses. "I must say, I was half expecting you to no-show."

"I wouldn't dare." Shocked he'd already judged me.

"It happens more than you think. People say they are going to show up, and they never do." He shook his head and leaned against the counter. "Regardless, you're here, and I'm glad for the company. You can set your things behind the counter. No cell phones while on shift, okay?"

"That's fair." It's not like I'd get a lot of calls anyway.

"Great. Then we'll get along fine. Here, grab this box, and I'll get the other."

A small grunt escaped my lips when I picked up the box. Not sure what was in the small box to make it so heavy.

"Follow me."

I half expected to need to walk around the building via the back alley, so I was pleasantly surprised to see a connecting door between his shop and the one next door. There was a definite chill in the room when we walked in, and despite the thick hoodie I shuddered in response.

Following Stanley's lead, I set the box at the head table.

The room was an empty store, complete with bare walls and windows. The solitary decoration in the yellowish room was the sign hanging in the picture window advertising the Grinch Tree workshop. The concrete floors were scattered with tables; twenty-one six-foot tables in three rows of seven. A few chairs sat stacked in the corner. Guess it was probably easier to walk around than sitting to make the trees.

Back into the floral shop, where it was noticeably warmer, Stanley went to the old-school coffee pot. He grabbed a mug and filled it, turning to me. "How do you like it?"

"Oh, umm, black is fine." I didn't see a fridge and wasn't a fan of powdered creamer. He handed it to me, and I wrapped my fingers around the mug. "Thanks."

"A good cup of coffee can help you muddle through the day. A great cup of coffee will get you through the worst day."

It was out there, but I nodded all the same and took a wee sip. There was a slightly familiar taste, but I couldn't put my finger on it.

"This is good."

"Make sure you let the coffee guy know."

"Who's that?" One of his suppliers, I supposed.

"The Coffee Loft. The guy there is trying out new flavours of beans and offered me a bag to sample. It's good. Something about it just brings back a memory."

That's why it was familiar. This was the stuff Carter was passing around his place the day I went crazy and tried to plan out a marketing campaign for him. I was such an idiot. As familiar as the flavour was, it was now going to be one I associated with my ridiculous overstepping.

"You know how to make coffee, right?"

I stared at the machine behind him. It couldn't be that hard. Add grounds to a basket with a filter, add water, and start. "I'm used to the single-serve variety, but this can be my first test. If I make a good cup, can I have a gold star?"

The old man cracked a weak smile. "I think I'm going to like working with you, Miss Cara."

Finally, something was going right for me.

"Okay, for tonight." Stanley went into detail about the supplies each table needed as he had a full workshop of twenty-one guests, and to make sure everything was there. He handed me an itemized list.

"If you have any questions, just ask. All the supplies are in the back room. And make sure to keep your cup filled." A weird request, but one I was all too happy to get behind.

First order of business was to look for the back room and familiarize myself with everything on the list. At a quick scan, I was going to need 22 of everything (since the head table needed stuff as well), and the list was long.

After a quick nod, I walked to the front of the store and looked for a shopping basket.

"There's a bin in the back you can use to haul supplies. But use the truck for the trees and make sure those are at each table before six."

"Before six. Sure thing."

I gave myself an introductory tour, although none of the items needed were in the display part of the store which was filled with plastic containers of fresh-cut flowers either out in the open or in the cooler. The only shelves with fresh greenery were of potted plants – perennials, or annuals or succulents (I hadn't the first clue) – but I was going to have to learn in a hurry if I was going to last for any length of time here.

The back room, which was larger than the store area, contained a giant walk-in cooler and a long table with shelves chock full of vases and flat cardboard pieces. It was here, I found most of the needed supplies tucked into a weathered box on the bottom of the table labeled in black marker *materials*. Interestingly enough, on the side was a shipping label, that when I scanned the return label, was from Daddy's shop. My heart squeezed at the connection.

Steeling myself and tucking away the memory of helping Dad in his store, I counted each identical item. I had most and scratched down how many of the others I needed on the back of my hand, but at least it was a start. I filled a bin with the smaller items and hauled it over, repeating the trip with the green foam forms, the containers, and five huge boxes of ornaments.

With an empty coffee cup in hand, I went to refill it behind the counter.

"So, I'm still missing a few things." I tipped the back of my hand to read the notes better.

"Like what?" Stanley hadn't removed his focus from the bundle of flowers he was currently wrapping a ribbon around.

"More wire cutters. There were only sixteen."

"Dang. Well, there's a storage closet beside the office. If there's none in there, people will have to share so space out the cutters. I'll make sure to grab a few from the hardware store next time I'm in the big city."

"There's no hardware store here?"

"Nope. Went out of business years back. Jillian's would likely sell something similar, but if Randall had two of them, I'd be surprised."

"Jillian's? That's the mish-mash store of all things, isn't it?"

"Clearly, you've been there." He chuckled and nodded. "Put your finger here."

I stuck my finger on the knot of red satin ribbon.

"Yeah, he sells a bit of everything but nothing I could really use, unfortunately. We need a hardware store here, but it'll never happen." With minimal effort, Stanley tied a postcard-worthy bow and snipped the ends to perfection. "Leave me a list of any other supplies we're missing, and I can grab those as well."

"And if I may, can I suggest the Preston-Wellex brand? They're comparable to the big brand names but about half the cost, and they'd be perfect for the gauge of wire you're using in the workshop. They're not as well-known mind you, but they're Canadian and they stand behind their products." It slipped out before I had control of my mouth.

"Know a little bit about tools, do ya?"

In a flash, heat seared my cheeks. "My dad used to own a hardware store back in Red Deer and I spent my evenings and weekends working there."

"And you went into marketing?" He lifted his hand into a stop position and studied me for a half-second. "No explanation. Not my place." Giving his attention back to the arrangement, he said, "Check the product closet. Key's on the hook in the office."

"Thank you."

Downing a large sip of coffee, I made my way back to the office and quickly spied the keys hanging by the door. It was even marked *closet.*

After a thorough scan, I didn't find any extra wire cutters, but I did find three more forms of the correct size, making sure to let him know the last one was being used.

With a full box of supplies, I juggled it on my hip and heavy-stepped back to the office to drop it off. I hadn't taken a good, long, and solid look before, but the tiny space was meticulous and super neat. On the wall beside his desk, I spotted a picture of a beautiful young lady in a frame resting on one of the shelves. It was tucked against the wall beside an ornate red vase with grooves etched into it.

Glancing around the space, I spied nothing even close to it. There weren't other framed pictures, and certainly, there weren't any vases. There wasn't even anything remotely floral or green. However, as much as the vase commanded my attention it was the framed picture beside it piquing my curiosity.

"That's my daughter," Stanley said.

I gasped and jumped, my face flooding with a high heat as if I'd been caught with my hand in the proverbial cookie jar.

With a steady hand, he pointed at the picture. "She died seven years ago on the operating bed after undergoing a standard gallbladder removal. Some freak thing they couldn't get under control. Sepsis I think?" He touched the container. "She was my Dahlia, and now she's here with me all the time."

I took a small step back but couldn't remove my eyes from the container. The harder I looked, the more intricate the etched detailing of a flower appeared, perhaps in the shape of her namesake?

"So there's a Daisy?"

"Her twin sister and my other daughter, yes. She and I had a falling out shortly after Dahlia's passing, and we haven't spoken since." His voice fell in the same slump as his shoulders. "She's living near my sister in Uxbridge, so she's keeping an eye on her and sends me updates."

"I'm sorry, that's tough. I know what it's like to lose family." With that, my gaze fell to the floor as he clapped me on the shoulder.

Losing family was the toughest thing ever, and my heart went out to him. Having living family members you didn't talk with was likely worse. They were around, and you knew it, and yet a part of your life but not really.

"Daisy's about your age, I suppose." He inched

back toward the main part of the store. "Whereas Daisy is the spring lover, or at least was, Dahlia loved this time of year and all things Christmas. Especially these Grinch trees. The workshop fee barely covers the costs, but I put it on every year just for her."

"Why don't you raise the prices a little? I'm sure no one would mind."

The soft snort made his nostrils flare. "It's a small town. Trust me. They would mind. Excessively." With an easy stride yet with a heavy clomping, he was back into the main area and putting a lid on top of a long box. "Truck's in the back." He nosed toward the back of the building. "Finish your coffee, and we'll start hauling in the trees." With a quick flick of his gaze, he stared at the analog clock on the wall just on top of the cooler. "Guests will start arriving shortly."

Finishing my coffee was easy – hauling in twenty-two mini trees and just as many pots, that was taxing. By the time I set the last one on the table, Stanley had unlocked the door on the workshop side and the guests started milling in. With the music playing softly, the smell of Christmas in the air, and the good-natured mingling going on, it sure felt like the magical holiday.

All I needed was to keep my focus, do a good job, and wait until my date on Saturday.

Karma, however, had other plans.

One of the last two people to arrive for the workshop was Bea. As I was refilling the coffee and getting a fresh pot going, my heart hammered to a complete stop as I locked on her. Her beautiful blue eyes narrowed into thinner slits until the doorbells overhead jingled.

Turning her head, I instinctively followed her gaze to the man entering a few steps behind.

As if she was watching a volleyball match, her gaze jumped back and forth between me and her younger brother, who was sporting a wee bit of a dour expression as he stomped into the place, kicking the snow off his boots. She cocked her brow and twisted to face him, hands on his shoulders ready to push him back out onto the sidewalk.

He stepped to the side, scanning the crowds until he connected with me. The frown flipped and as his head moved in a slow bob, a giant smile formed.

Chapter Eleven

PUSHING THROUGH THE twenty other guests, Carter wove his way over to stand before me. One long, steady gaze down and back up was enough to take away any chill I may have had.

"I know when you said earlier that perhaps I'd see you sooner than Saturday, I had no idea it would be tonight." He shoved his hands into the pockets of his jeans, something I hadn't seen him wear before as he always wore smart chinos or almost dress pants. Jeans were a first, but if things hadn't changed, I bet they put a lot of focus still on the rear view.

Shaking the thought from my head, I tried to hide my growing nervousness. Seeing him at my place of work, especially on my first day, it sent a flurry of butterflies swirling.

My mouth went dry, and proper words disappeared from my vocabulary.

"You're helping Stanley?" His left brow lowered enough to shadow his dark eyes. "Do you two know each other? Or were you passing by and just decided on a whim to help, because that sounds more like the Cara I know."

I shrugged and plastered an innocent smile on my face. "You are partially correct. I saw the workshop help wanted sign and figured why not?"

Of course, Stanley chose to walk by right then. It was an innocent enough statement, but would he think the worst? I swallowed down a lump of guilt for not having checked the area before opening my mouth.

Carter took the bait. "Wait, you work here now?"

"Hired until the end of the year."

"But where are you staying?"

Stanley walked to the head table and lowered the music slightly, my cue to get back to the job at hand, making sure the coffee pot was always full, and offering assistance when needed.

Carter nodded. "We'll talk after."

"Alright, ladies and gentlemen. Thank you for

attending." Stanley went into detail about how tonight was going to work and set about explaining things, while I slithered against the back of the room, flipping my gaze between the coffee pot and Carter.

Carter sauntered back to a table in the middle, each step commanding my undivided attention.

Occasionally, throughout the workshop, he'd tip his head toward Beatrice before they both would turn to glance at me. It was an odd sensation; I felt like I was being watched with every footstep I took; his was pleasurable, hers as cold as ice.

However, there were nineteen others to hold my attention and I made sure to circle the room, with a quick stop at the coffee pot just for good measure.

With the music volume turned up, the room came alive with the fresh scent of snipped cedar, and a group in the far corner started singing along with the music. People happily wrapped wire around the trees and laughed out loud when the ornament wouldn't stay attached and kept flinging to the table behind. Overall, the mood was jovial, and, like a suitable server, I went around refilling everyone's coffee to keep their spirits going.

Every customer I talked to, or complimented

on the way they added just the right amount of greenery to the bottom, I couldn't help myself and I stole a glance to Carter. As much as I wanted to go over and offer whatever blind assistance I could, or just basically chat about the project, I couldn't make my feet move toward him. Pretty sure it was the questioning and icy glare from Beatrice holding me back.

The two workshop hours went by in a snap and the happy, festive crowds started dispersing, leaving a handful still hanging around. Carter took his tree outside, leaving Bea standing with hers, staring intently in my direction. Honestly, I think she spent more time staring at me than she did working on her project, and the minimal decorations along the base and around the tree were proof. The others in the room were way more elaborate.

A small group had gathered around Stanley so to avoid her glare, I decided to get the cleanup started early and grabbed the broom, sweeping from the far corner.

Beatrice wasn't to be deterred and click-clacked over in her heels, shifting her minimalist tree to her hip. "I've heard you've made a few visits here."

Assuming the *here* meant Ridge Heights in

general and not Daisy and Dahlia's, I swept some cedar clippings and ribbon cuttings into a pile, refusing to make eye contact. Hatred oozed out of her and I tried, unsuccessfully, sweeping the mess into my growing pile as well.

Her voice lowered and clipped words jumped out. "Stay away from Carter. He's been through enough and doesn't need you breaking his heart again. You did enough damage the last time."

With that, I cracked my head up in record time and stomped the broom. "Excuse me?"

"You heard me." Her lips puckered into a thin line. "Stay away from him. Far away. You're already affecting him, and that's not good."

The bells overhead jingled, and I tossed my frazzled attention to the target of our conversation. Carter's jovial look fell and shaking his head, he stormed over.

"Bea?" That question held so much power.

"What?" She turned away so I couldn't see her face and therefore whatever expression she was giving her younger brother, but based on the tone, it was sugary sweet. "I was just welcoming Cara since it's been a while since I last saw her. I've heard she's been a regular visitor and I thought it was nice to finally say hello." Her face morphed as she faced me; one perfectly manicured eyebrow shot halfway up her forehead while at the same time her eyes narrowed. I'd never watched a face change like that; it was chilling, to say the least.

Carter looked at me, and I didn't know how to react or what to say. So many thoughts and questions were storming through my head.

How had I broken his heart? He'd been the one to let me go. He did the damage, not me.

Also, what did she mean he's been through a lot?

Bea spun around. "Let's go, Carter." She tugged on his arm.

"Give me a minute. I'll meet you outside."

"I think we should get going." Her clipped words were like nails on a chalkboard.

"I've started your car. It'll be warm enough for you, and I said I'll be right there." His words sputtered through gritted teeth.

Not only did that sound raise the hairs on the back of my neck, but it also caused Bea to back up.

"If it's too much trouble, just go home. Honestly, I can walk." He tugged a toque out of his pocket and slammed it onto his head. The utter defiance almost made me giggle. Almost.

"Whatever." She stalked to the door.

"Oh, hey, Bea," he called out over the few people mingling nearby. The sauciness in his voice vanished into the air. "Are you waiting for me? Or am I walking?"

"Of course, I'll wait." With that, the bells jingled once more, and she stepped outside.

He shook his head. "I'd apologise for her, but sadly, you know what she's like."

As much as I wanted to focus on him, I stared at the door, positive she was standing out in the cold watching us through the window.

"Back to my earlier question." His voice was so soft and sweet, it pulled me right back to look up into his face.

"And that would be?" I still had questions of my own, so I didn't remember what his original question had been.

"So, you've moved here? Where are you staying?" He stared deep into my eyes, so much curiosity hidden in the depths.

"Motor Inn on Alpine Way."

He scrunched his face together. "That's not the best part of town and not the greatest place to stay."

I playfully punched his arm. "Well, they have a charger for Casper." A confused look briefly crossed his face. "The Batmobile?"

A solid head bop happened. "Ah, yes. Your friendly ghost."

"Plus, they rent the rooms out by the week—"

"Eww… that can't be sanitary."

I shrugged. "It's not by the hour and besides, it seems clean."

He leaned closer and whispered in my ear. "Wash all the dishes before you eat off them."

Wanting to shrug off the suggestion, I instead nodded, somewhat worried about why the heads up on the dishes. "It's temporary since I'm not sure how long I'll be here…"

"Why not?"

"Depends on a few things, I suppose." I squared my shoulders and readied myself for his response. Aside from the fact I only had five weeks of a job ahead of me…

"Like what?" His head tipped curiously to the side, and he widened his stance.

"Well, if I'm being honest, you." My breath froze as I waited for him to say something. Anything.

My heart beat faster as my lungs burned until he finally spoke. "That puts a lot of pressure on a guy like me."

"Well… yes… I guess it does." But I wasn't

sorry. Not yet.

A broad smile appeared, curving his lips gently upward. "A challenge I can most definitely step up for, right?"

"Game on then?"

"Game on."

From the corner of my eye, I spotted Stanley hovering. "I need to go."

"Guess I'll be seeing you around."

"Saturday night for sure, and who knows, maybe even before that?"

"I'd like that." He gave me a friendly wave and headed for the door. "Thanks for sharing out the coffee, Stanley. You're mugnificent."

Quickly he assessed the coffee station and replied with a smile. "It seemed like a hit. I have nothing left."

"I'll bring a few packages tomorrow." With a wave goodbye, Carter left the shop.

Stanley ambled over with a tired limp in his steps and locked the door once the last workshop customer exited. "That was a fun night."

"It was."

I resumed my sweeping, slightly embarrassed I had been caught chatting on the job. It was like being fifteen all over again and working at the local ice cream shop. The boss had been strictly adamant about not standing around. He didn't pay for conversation; he paid for a sparkling clean restaurant and happy customers, and in that order.

Stanley cleared his throat. "When I asked you to make sure the coffee was filled, I simply meant the pot, not for you to go around serving everyone. They are more than capable of refilling their own Styrofoam cups." He grabbed a couple of used cups and dropped them into the garbage. A deep building smirk tugged on the side of his mouth. "However, I know they appreciated it, as did I having an extra set of hands around. You done good tonight, Kid."

I swallowed. That was the most praise I'd received on a job in a really long time, even jerkish Tory never complimented my work, and I'd been there for nearly two years. "Thank you."

"Benson would be proud."

"How'd you know?"

He leaned against a table. "I'm old, but I can piece a puzzle together."

"I never…"

His weathered and calloused hand swiped through the air. "We weren't friends or anything, Gallagher and I, but he ran an honest business until he closed shop. When you started talking tools, well, I put two and two together."

Tears welled in my eyes.

"Nah, nah, none of that here." He spun around and with the rag, wiped off the coffee station. "I'm running another workshop tomorrow night and Thursday night, and I'd love to have your help." He straightened and turned. "Last workshop is on Friday night, and I'll be getting you to run it while I finish up the work for the tree lighting ceremony on Saturday. You good with that?"

I gulped and tightened my grip on the broom handle. "I've never run a workshop before."

"You'll get the feel for it. It's not hard, and there's no wrong way for them to mess it up." Laughing, he bent down to swipe a twig off the floor. "Well, this may be the wrong way." He dropped it into the garbage. "But it's more up your alley than mine. You seem like a people person."

"Thank you, Sir."

"Stanley. Please call me that and not sir."

"Yes." I nodded, knowing better. "Thank you for the offer. I can," I inhaled sharply, "I'd be honoured to run your workshop on Friday night."

"Great. Finish sweeping in here and shut the lights off when you're done. I'll be next door finishing up some paperwork. Leave me a list of things you need as I'll be in town tomorrow grabbing supplies." Steps from the flower shop side, his big frame halted in the doorway. "It's none of my business, but when you said you was leaving your city life behind, was it because you were running away from problems or running to them?" He shook his head and waved a hand through the air. "You know what, don't answer that." About to step into the shop, he dropped his head. "On second thought…" He ran his thick fingers through his grey strands. "About Carter, do me a favour and go easy on him. He's a solid guy but he's … Well, just be kind is all."

That was the second warning I'd gotten about Carter. Time for me to roll up my sleeves and do some digging.

Chapter Twelve

MY DIGGING WAS fruitless. Googling *Carter Cross* provided little to no information. He had to have signed an NDA or some other privacy document with the overseas schools as there was no mention of him. Like zero. No debate team captain. No moral ethics committee member. Not even a hint of participation in a low-budget drama production.

His online presence was even more mysterious. No social media pages and nothing about his travels to the coffee bean capital of the world either. It was like he was the real-life version of Casper the Ghost.

All I could find was his name on a link to the Coffee Loft page, which was understandable since he currently worked there. Everything else was a mystery. How was that possible? Even Googling my name produced several hits to pages other than my locked-down social media accounts, which actually caused me great concern. Was my temporary six-week stint at a minor league marketing firm really worthy of internet knowledge? I highly doubted it was.

How was Carter able to avoid all that?

It baffled my fragile mind and gave me more questions than I could find answers to. Which I detested. I hated that he was this enigma, and not just to me, but to the whole world. Lack of communication was one of my many pet peeves, so I promised myself, the next time I saw him, which I hoped was before our big Tree Lighting ceremony date, I was just going to come out and ask.

PERUSING THE AISLES of the grocery store on an empty stomach, I was in desperate need of something other than vending machine food or the yummy add-it-to-my-waistline foods from the Coffee Loft, and absolutely everything looked worthy. However, I needed nutrition, but also easy-to-prepare foods since the kitchenette wasn't loaded with all the comforts of my appliances still tucked into the cabinets back in my apartment.

The produce clerk, or perhaps the manager, was unpacking a box of not-quite-ripe bananas and setting them on the stand. Craning my neck, I scanned them looking for ready-to-eat ones. The ones on display were still firm and green.

"Can I help you?"

I scrunched my nose and continued to search. "Don't suppose you have any that are ripe and ready-to-eat?"

"I'm sure I can find you something." He gave me a hopeful wink, but it produced a small involuntary shudder inside. Squatting, he pulled out another box, setting it with ease on top of the other crate with a slight grunt.

"Heavy?" Although I wasn't sure why I asked. I honestly didn't care.

"Oh no. I lift things like this all the time." The playful smirk matched the wiggle he did.

I half expected him to flex his arms, but thankfully he didn't. Instead, he grabbed a bunch of market-ready bananas, and handed it to me, staring at my hand.

"Thanks." I took off the three I wanted and set the rest down. When he gave me a curious look, I jumped to answer. "For baking. It was all I needed."

"Banana bread? If so, we have riper bananas in

the back I can grab you."

"This is fine, thanks."

He leaned on the top of the boxes, completely casual in his stance. "You sure? It's no trouble at all for you miss."

"Honestly, this is all I need." I added them to my cart and whipped two Granny Smith apples off the nearby display.

"Here, let me help you pick the best ones." Another wink.

I backed up, putting the cart between me and the produce guy.

"Oh, there you are," Carter said to me as he roamed over and slipped a small-sized dishwashing liquid soap under the three bananas. "Hey, Patrick."

"Carter." Patrick's gaze volleyed between him and me. "Are you…?"

He didn't answer, merely raised both brows.

"Oh, well." He paled slightly, and with a quick spin on his heels, he shuffled to the display of fresh veggies.

"Hey," I said, playfully bumping Carter as we stepped further away from the banana display, super grateful for the interception.

Bundled up in a thick winter jacket, I was pretty sure he barely felt the nudge but the lazy smile suggested otherwise.

"What's up with this?" I pulled the dishwashing liquid out and waved it around, tossing a quick glance back to Patrick, who was now busy talking to an older lady about carrots.

"Trust me on this. You'll need it."

"You make it sound like the place is a dump. It's not that bad."

He held on to the side of my grocery cart, looking cool, calm, and collected. Plus, he smelled like a fresh shower with a hint of spicy cologne. "Why stay there though?"

"It was all that's available."

"There are several vacant homes for rent and lofts above the main drag."

Which were higher priced than I was ready to dish out for this temporary shift in living accommodations. "If things stabilize, it may be something I'll look into, but for now, this is the best I can do and all I can afford."

"The best you can do? I know you better than that. And all you can afford? With a little digging, you can find something slightly higher priced and far more comfortable." The air crackled between us as he locked his gaze on me, sending my pulse absolutely atmospheric. "Tell you what, why don't you stay at my place?"

A million scenarios sped through my head, and all the possibilities I'd dreamed of lit up in quick succession. My pulse raced as my breath held tight.

"I can move in temporarily with Bea, who has a massive place on the other side of the highway, so it's no biggie." He rocked on his feet, totally oblivious to my crashlanding flight of fancy.

What was wrong with me? Why did I have to jump to the far end of an idea?

"I... ah." Glancing at the few groceries I had set into the kid's seat of the cart, I reorganized them into an order which ended up squishing a fresh tomato.

He pulled back and twisted his head, eyes narrowing just a hint. "Wait a sec, you didn't think?"

"Good grief, no. I was just taken aback that you'd offer such a thing." I stumbled over my words as I waved my hand frantically through the air. "I mean, we're still not... And... well, we haven't really..."

The light chuckle rolling out of him did nothing to settle my electrified nerves. "You're cute when your face fills with blood."

I fanned my sweater, feeling hotter than when

I'd bask in the sunshine on the shorelines of Sylvan Lake. "Yeah, well…"

I pushed my cart over to the raspberries and flipped over a few packages. For the cost, one would think they'd be better looking and not sporting tiny tips of mold. The adrenaline spike was fading, leaving my hands all shaky, and I set the package down and wrapped my hands around the handle of the cart.

"So, I'm deeply curious." He cleared his throat, grabbing my attention. "How long have you been in town?"

We walked side-by-side as if it were the most natural thing in the world.

"I moved here two days ago, and last night was my first work night at Daisy & Dahlia's."

"Wow, fresh move, and for some reason, I figured you've been here longer." He grabbed a bag of oranges, sight unseen, and dropped them into his basket.

We sauntered out of the produce area, and over to the bakery where they had to have been pumping the scent of fresh bread into the air. It was like a drug following my nose over.

"No, just been a frequent visitor." Quite frequent. "But time for a change. Things weren't working out in Red Deer, and so far, this has been interesting."

"No regrets?" He grabbed a bag of cinnamon raisin bagels and tossed them into my cart. "I know you like them."

I stared at the six-pack of bagels, shocked he remembered. I'd mentioned it maybe once in college. "It's been two days, there hasn't been time for regrets."

He smirked, the right side of his face pushing against his cheek. "Just checking. You tend to be impulsive."

"But I've never regretted anything." Which was true. I was impulsive. It was how I ran my life, and so far, it was good, but was it ideal?

I stopped pushing my cart as the weight of it all dug into my shoulders causing me to rest my forearms on the handle and take a deep breath.

"You okay?"

A languishing sigh escaped as I roamed my eyes over his unzipped jacket, over the glitter of his gold necklace, and up to meet his gaze. "Am I too young to have a mid-life crisis?"

Head tipped back, he started laughing but stopped suddenly and closed the gap between us. "You're serious?"

"Yeah."

A few people stared at us, and I pulled further into my knee-length coat.

"Is that what you're thinking? That you're having a mid-life crisis? You're barely thirty. C'mon."

I shrugged and stared at the random groceries and at the weird bottle of dish-washing liquid. "Look at my life. Nothing over the last month has been stable, and here I am, moved to a new place, living in a motel, and working for a florist. So not what I set out to do with my life."

"Life is funny, isn't it?"

"Only funny in the ironic ha-ha way, but there's nothing funny about job instability and relocation."

Carter put his hand on my shoulder. "Look at it like this, you're young enough to reset your life. Do what you dare to dream. Rewrite your destiny."

I cocked an eyebrow and planted a hand firmly on my hip. "Is that what you're doing?"

He shook his head, the blond strands flailing out to the sides. "Sometimes practicality calls for settlement. I'm doing what I need to for right now." There was a sharp inhale. "And to answer your question before you ask, yes, I'm mostly happy."

"Mostly?"

"Who do you know that's all the way happy?" He took off toward the dairy cases.

Good point.

I shuffled through my incredibly small list of friends and acquaintances, and yeah, none of them were truly happy. Everyone was dealing with something to weigh them down. Was true happiness unattainable? It was the ultimate, yet unreachable, goal?

Dragging my feet, I followed him and added a slim carton of milk to my small pile of food. It wasn't much, but then again, the fridge in the motel was one of those snack-sized ones and wouldn't hold much. Topping up with two containers of yogurt, I was nearly done. It was pathetic but would have to do.

"Set your basket in the cart," I told him, seeing as how his basket was overflowing.

"Thanks, but then I need to push." He hip-checked me out of the way after he set his basket into the cart and took control. "You don't have much. What else do you need?"

"Easy to microwave staples, since that's all there is, aside from a tiny fridge. Of the two-burner stove, only one element works, which is fine. I'm not making fancy meals."

"You're not proving your case with this motel being all you claim."

"It'll be fine. You'll see."

Under his watchful eye, I grabbed a few non-perishables to add to my small but manageable stash as we small talked about the town and the upcoming tree-lighting ceremony. The more he talked about it, the more I was excited about checking it out. However, I needed to secure a pair of skates first.

After we each paid for our groceries, he escorted me out to my car and loaded my two bags into the backseat, leaving his in the cart.

I leaned against my door. "Thanks for shopping with me. It was great seeing you again."

In a move I did not expect, he braced his arms against the car on either side of me. "Have lunch with me?"

"Are you asking or telling me?" I rather liked how some switch had been turned on inside of him; it was a spark I remembered him having back in our youth.

"Both." His gaze danced between my eyes and lowered briefly to my lips.

I stared into his dark browns and blinked him into focus, barely breathing as I whispered, "Love to."

Chapter Thirteen

THE CAR ROLLED to a stop outside my motel door, in front of the no parking sign. I only planned on being a couple of minutes, just long enough to throw my groceries in the tiny fridge and skedaddle, surely bylaw officers weren't that fast here.

"I'll be just a hot minute."

I fiddled with the display and put the games on the screen. Amanda always enjoyed playing them whenever I'd get my tires swapped.

"Oh, no thanks." He remembered how to open the door, something I remember taking me a few attempts to master. "I need to see this place of yours."

"Really?" I cringed as I remembered the state of disaster I'd left it in this morning.

"Yup."

He helped carry the bags and leaned against the wall as I stuck my key in.

"It's not tidy."

"I promise I won't judge."

"I would."

The door squealed and creaked as it opened. Addressing that was next on my list. In the meantime, I had a mountain of embarrassment to deal with as my clothes and tools were scattered everywhere, and I prayed he didn't need a bathroom. My bras were hanging over the shower bar.

"Let me just toss these things away." I practically wrestled the bag from him, dumped the contents on the counter, and shoved them as quick as I could into the tiny fridge, hip-checking it for good measure to ensure it sealed – item four to fix. "Alright, let's go."

I grabbed his hand and started pulling him to the door as there was absolutely no need to linger.

"Let me just check."

No. But like watching a car crash, I couldn't not watch as he grabbed a couple of dishes from the dry rack and scrutinized them, tipping them to and fro.

"I swear they're clean."

"You took my advice?"

"Of course." *It came from you.*

As he continued to scan, and most likely judge, I scurried around, picking up my clothes and depositing them on the available chair. The tools remained in a pile on the floor.

"I need to catch up on laundry."

"There's a laundromat around the corner, down the stairs in the basement." He pointed to the left, but inside the motel room, which wasn't facing the main road, I wasn't sure where that was. No doubt, Google would help. "I'm trying to get them to carry our coffee, so if you go there, mind putting in a good word?"

"Of course."

He kicked at the toolbox near the cupboard door. "What are you working on?"

"Nothing."

The cupboard door wasn't level and therefore wasn't closing properly. A few quick adjustments and it was perfect. How I wished I'd put my tools and level away. Mind you, I didn't think I'd be bringing anyone back.

"Can we go now?" I stood by the door, desperate to pick up from where we ended in the parking lot of the grocery store.

"Sure, why not?" There was an odd skip in his steps. "You getting hungry?"

I stopped in a heartbeat and stared into his eyes. "You have no idea."

"Oh, really?" There was just enough fire in his gaze to ignite my embers.

"Let's go."

With my groceries safely stowed in my motel room, I drove Carter to his place and parked alongside the road, helping him carry his up the stairs at the back of the building. The metal-grated stairs were outside, and looking up from the back to his place, I would've never guessed they would've led to an apartment. It looked rather industrial.

We climbed the twenty or so steps, and after we closed the door, he shrugged out of his jacket and hung it in a tiny closet. Not that I blamed him for removing his jacket; it was toasty warm which was apparent the second the door opened, and a burst of heat slammed into us.

"Wow, you like it warm, eh?"

"Who doesn't?" He nodded and took a grocery bag from my hand. "You can hang your jacket there."

I spun around and tucked behind the door was an ornamental coat rack. Adding my coat to it, I paced around and checked out his spacious apartment. In addition to the place being borderline hot, it also had a slight tropical scent to it, something spicy yet citrus-like. I loved it. It took me back in time to when we were younger, and he always had a mandarin orange fragrance tree hanging in his car.

"I'll put on some tea and get these put away. Have a seat and make yourself comfortable."

His couch had a navy-blue waffle-weave blanket thrown across it, as if he'd had a guest who vacated in a rush, and the living room wasn't as neat and tidy as I thought it'd be. The Carter of our younger years always had a meticulously clean bedroom.

Sidestepping a pile of books, I beelined to the bookcase as I'd read somewhere if you wanted to know someone, you checked out their bookshelves. Aside from a few trinkets (nothing even coffee-related), a collection of video games, and a smattering of Blu-rays, there wasn't much of interest. He had a couple of family pictures – one which included his parents and all the sisters, another with spouses and one tiny human, which I assumed was Starcy, his niece. With an upturned nose and a smattering of freckles, she was adorable.

The books weren't stacked lovingly on the shelves, but rather in piles on his coffee table. One stack was a full collection of BJ Sutcliff novels with a sticky note and the words *island author* scratched across. Another pile contained names I didn't immediately recognize but tickled the back of my brain like they should have been familiar.

It wasn't the stack of books or the bookshelves devoid of reading material that caught my eye though – his walls were filled with artwork, but mostly huge, green leafy trees and in one of them a guy was holding onto the branch of berries. Or was it cherries?

I tapped the one picture and called out to Carter. "Are these those coffee trees you talked about?"

He wiped his hand on a towel, which he then threw over his shoulder as he walked into the living room. "Yep. That there is my friend Diego."

"The plantation worker?" Our conversation came back with impressive speed, and internally, I clapped myself on the back for remembering. Carter nodded. "Wow, that's cool. So that's where coffee comes from, eh?" I laughed at my words, unsure why it sounded funny to say that.

"They're pretty, aren't they? I can't wait to go back and work again with Diego. Some day." He tipped his head toward the kitchen. "When you're done admiring, come keep me company while I make us lunch."

"Sure thing. Can I use the bathroom first?"

"Down the hall."

There were three doors. One was too small, like a closet door, the other was half-cracked, and a quick peek told me it was his bedroom with an unmade bed and the curtains pulled open just enough to allow a sliver of sunlight in. As much as I wanted to explore, I didn't and took to the other open door – belonging to a bathroom that clearly wasn't anticipating company.

There were gobs of toothpaste in the sink, droplets of dried water on the mirror, and spilled contact lens solution which had dried to a white finish, something I personally was guilty of not immediately wiping up. His medicine chest was half open, and as I strained my head to steal a view without fully opening the door for fear it would creak loudly like my own, it wasn't hard to miss the array of orange pill bottles in a variety of sizes on half of the shelves.

That was a lot of medications.

I shook my head and whispered, "No peeking."

But my hand twitched and reached for the tiny

mirror to pull it back for a better look. A slow squeak scratched out from the rusted hinge. What was he taking all the pills for?

A knock sounded against the door, and I stifled a scream.

"Oh my goodness, Cara, I just remembered what condition the bathroom is in, and I'm so sorry for the mess. Please don't hold it against me." His voice was full of shame.

"Don't scare me like that." My heart pounded as I shook my head, confident he was waiting for a response. "Nah, it's fine. It looks like mine."

"I highly doubt that."

In haste, I sat on the toilet and did my business, totally feeling like I'd been caught with my hand in the proverbial cookie jar even though I hadn't fully studied what was hiding in the cabinet, but there wasn't time.

Flushing, I stood and washed my hands, stealing a glance at my face. Yep, I had guilt sprayed all over it, and I tipped my head from side to side while blinking rapidly to help dimmish the look. It failed.

Shoulders back, I opened the door, for some reason thinking Carter was still there, and readied myself for his questioning gaze or curious smirk.

Instead, I padded down the hall to join him in the kitchen where he was chopping a green pepper.

He kept his head down. "I wasn't expecting company. I'm sorry."

"It's okay." I took a seat at the counter, watching the way his hand effortlessly cut through the pepper like a skilled chef. "What can I help with?"

"I'm not making anything fancy, just a market omelette and toast, if that works for you?" He looked up through his long lashes but mostly kept his chin tucked down. "Unless you'd rather have Mini Wheats. I have a bowl, milk, and an hour to kill." The words breezed out with a grin.

"You remember?" I leaned closer.

He set the knife down and rested both his palms on the counter. "How could I forget? Watching you drop one, maybe two, Mini Wheats at a time into the bowl of milk before you scooped them up with your spoon. You didn't even drop the next ones in until you'd finished chewing."

"Of all the things to remember about me." I shook my head. There were other, much better memories he could've – and should've – clung to.

"One of your most endearing." He tipped his head back down as he grabbed the knife to resume chopping, but I didn't miss the pink colour gently tinting the outer limits of his beard. "Please tell me you still eat them, and that's how you still consume them because I didn't see a box of cereal in your shopping cart?"

"Of course. They get soggy otherwise." I shifted in my seat and crossed my legs. "You know, my last boyfriend dumped me because of the way I ate my cereal. Said I was like a serial killer."

"A cereal killer? As in c-e-r-e-a-l?" He burst out laughing and popped his head up, searching my eyes until he tickled my soul. "Guess it's a good thing you're not still together because that's a Cara Trademark, don't ever lose that." The pepper consumed his attention once more. "Or ever stop being you because of some guy."

"Oh, I'm not afraid to be me."

"Good." He slid the chopped greens into a bowl. "So yes to the market omelet?"

I craned my neck out and peered into the bowl. "I have no idea what *a market omelette* is, but it sounds good."

"It's made with all the produce you'd find at a market – peppers, eggs, diced back bacon, and a sprinkling of Monterey jack cheese."

"Sounds good. Sign me up." I watched the

muscles on his forearm tense and relax as he cubed slices of thick back bacon and added them to the bowl. "Can I make us a coffee?"

He shrugged. "Sure. Grinder's beside the machine. Pods are in the basket underneath. Use the bag marked NB."

"NB?"

"It's a new blend I'm working on."

"You're really into this whole make-your-own coffee beans experience, aren't you?" I opened the bag and took a solid whiff. Holy beans... what was it about the scent of coffee that soothed the soul?

"Wait until you grind them." He'd stood beside me, shoulder to shoulder, and took the bag from my hand, pouring a few beans into the coffee grinder. A loud whirring noise filled the space as the beans were pulverized, smashed, and turned into a fine grind. After a few seconds, he pulled off the lid and held it under my nose.

I inhaled deeply as I looked into his eyes. "That's amazing."

"Right?"

We stood there with the fresh scent of coffee hanging between us. The longer I stayed locked on his gaze, the harder and faster my heart started to pound. He swallowed and gave his lips a quick lick, and just like that, I was back to being a giddy eighteen-year-old, staring up into the eyes of my first love, and he was staring back, his gaze wrapping around my heart and lassoing me closer.

He set the grinder on the counter and then gently cupped my face, tipping his head to the side as he leaned down and hovered over my lips. His thumbs stroked my cheeks, and I closed my eyes to the electrified sensations zooming down off my face and circulating through my body. His breath was sweet and warm and yet there was no contact. Glancing at what I hoped wasn't disappointment, I brushed open my eyes. His were closed, but his face was tight. Instead, he leaned his forehead against mine, and a surge of disappointment swelled inside my heart.

"What? That's it?" I asked, the words unable to be blocked. Anger won out.

"Cara, I can't." With that, he dropped his hands and backed away.

"No!" I slammed my hand on the counter, letting the sting reverberate through my arm. "You need to stop doing this. You need to stop running away."

He snapped his gaze to lock onto mine.

"Is it because of the meds in your bathroom?"

The Adam's Apple bobbed with impressive strength.

"What are you hiding? And why on this good green earth does your sister think *I* broke up with *you*?"

"Because to save face, that's what I told her." His head dropped between the arms he braced on the counter. A long, lingering sigh breathed out, deflating him.

"I want answers, Carter. I think I deserve them."

"Then sit, and I'll explain."

Sitting on the stool, my foot bounced long enough that my other leg was losing feeling. As he avoided my gaze and added grounds to each pod, and then filled the reservoir with tap water, he finally pressed the large cup button.

My anger hadn't abated, despite folding my arms across my chest so tightly to control my breathing. No doubt, if there was a mirror nearby, my nostrils would've been flaring. I desperately needed to get my emotions under control.

He said nothing, but his shoulders sagged, and his back rolled outward until finally the first cup was ready. "Are you sure you want to hear this?"

Heat dropped out of my face and despite the

warmth of the room, I shuddered.

"You're not..." I could barely say the word, and I flashed back to the way my father had announced his bump to the front of Heaven's line. "Oh my." My heart pounded louder than the words. "You're not dying, are you?"

Chapter Fourteen

I WASN'T SURE if I could handle any kind of tragic news, and neither did my body as my eyes flooded with tears. An anxiety I'd kept at bay for the past five years reared its ugly head.

"Cara." He reached for my freezing hand, and tenderly stroked it with his warm thumb. "First off, I'm not dying. Not by a long shot."

The tears broke their hold and streamed down my cheeks with impressive force of relief. "Oh, thank goodness."

For just a moment, I was terrified how after having reconnected with him, I was going to lose him all over again. Forever this time. It was too much to accept, and yet hearing how he wasn't dying, still didn't put me completely at ease.

Something else was still up. That tight, contorted expression held more words than the stack of books on his coffee table and floor.

Without reservation, he pulled me into a hug, and I rested the side of my face against his sweater.

"Please tell me what's going on." I sniffed as my voice cracked.

"Let me start at the beginning."

A cool gush of air swooped between us as I straightened up to take him all in.

"While in Scotland, I started having these weird… episodes."

I leaned closer, my breath catching in the back of my throat as I uncrossed my legs. "What kind of episodes?"

Aimlessly, he rubbed at his beard, finding a spot just below his chin to focus on. "I'd just go blank and stare off into space, but not like being in a zone or anything, like you'd sometimes get when you'd be deep in thought. My roommate said it was super weird as these episodes would happen mid-conversation as I'd just stop talking in the middle of a sentence. Kicker was, I never remembered doing it. Thought it was something in the air."

I raised a questionable brow.

"Yeah, dumb, I know that now. After a year in

the UK, I transferred to Switzerland."

I remembered – it was incredibly hard and looking back, it was the start of when our communications grew distant. Whereas it had been days between emails and phone calls, the distance painfully grew to a week, and then longer.

"Then one day, after one of these spells in the auditorium, I started shaking uncontrollably and the professor called for medical help."

I swallowed, terrified the loud sound would cause Carter to stop talking, but it didn't. Leaning in closer after I wiped away my tears, I continued listening with all my heart.

"They ran a few tests at the hospital, a lot in fact, and it turns out I have adult-onset epilepsy. I am one of those who didn't develop it from a brain infection, or a prenatal injury. Mine seemed to be triggered by a genetic abnormality which kicked in."

Over and over again, I replayed his words in my head. *Adult-onset epilepsy.* My gaze wandered all around the kitchen, jumping from the stove to the canister of utensils to the Keurig machine and back to settle over his handsome face – the one staring at me, begging me to say or do something.

My skin tingled with a slight discomfort, and

my voice warbled to nearly inaudible levels. "Epilepsy? Why didn't you tell me?"

"I wanted to, believe me, but I couldn't. I had a tough time understanding it all myself. It was so much to take in, a whirlwind of testing, and in such a short time too." He looked away as he shrugged. "I started spiralling down a dark hole and shut myself off from the world. I didn't know how else to handle the change, and the worst part was I didn't know how to tell *you*. I couldn't just drop the diagnosis on you, like it was dropped on me. It was... I was... it wasn't the best of situations."

Reaching out, I held on tight to his hand. "I would've understood. Oh my gosh, Carter, you were so far away from all of us. I would've dropped everything and rushed over to be with you, to have supported you through all those tests, and been a second set of ears to hear everything the doctors said. I loved you so much, there wouldn't have been anything I wouldn't have done for you."

"You loved me?"

Yeah, that's what he was going to take away from my sentence. Typical Carter.

His head bobbed, and he sighed loudly as a weak smile tickled and then faded on the edge of his lips. "I know that now, and maybe back then, I knew you would've been what I needed, but I was just so scared and unsettled, I didn't know what else to do, so I did what I knew best – I retreated."

Which, ironically, I understood all too well.

When Dad died, despite everyone's incessant offer to help in any way they could, I refused and pulled into myself. I couldn't move. I couldn't breathe. I didn't know how to live in a world where my dad wasn't a part of it.

After a while, and after my standardized rejections, friends stopped calling and reaching out. When I truly needed them the most, even just a quick hello to let me know they hadn't given up on me, they had in fact abandoned me. I'd never felt so alone.

Is that what Carter had felt?

"I would've supported you and taken care of you. I still would." I reached for his hand which had chilled slightly.

Inch by inch, his gaze searched my face and touched the edges of my soul. "I didn't want you to be watching my every move, watching for the moment when I'd get a blank look, ready to help me when I had a seizure."

My shoulders slumped, also understanding *that* all too well. Dad had been the same way, and despite his objections, I did watch his every move. He even called me his little mother hen as I couldn't help myself; it was a natural thing to do. How in the world could I ever stop feeling?

As I sat there, clipped sentences that wanted to be given life stayed stagnant, and I recalled previous moments, searching our latest history for something I may have missed. Something he may have hidden from me.

The metaphorical lightbulb went on and my mouth remembered how to vocalise my thoughts.

"Wait a second. That second day I met you in the Coffee Loft when you handed me a sample and you sat with me for a few minutes. You suddenly got all weird and jumped up and disappeared. Were you having, or were you about to—"

He cut me off before I finished, and his blond hairs flew through the air as his head dropped. "Yes, I was about to have a seizure."

Holy. Cow.

All that time I'd selfishly thought it was about me, even when he had said it wasn't. My heart splintered knowing he'd been hiding his painful secrets from me for years.

Tenderly holding his hand in mine, I rubbed the top. "Does it happen often?"

"Lately, it's been happening more frequently."

"Because of me." It wasn't a question; it was something Bea had said – how I was *affecting* him.

The darkness in his eyes deepened. "Absolutely not. Why would you say that?"

The words took on a tone of their own. "Something your sister said."

A low growl roared out of him. "What did she say? Exactly."

"That I was affecting you. How I'd broken your heart once before, and I needed to stay away." I snorted at the memory.

"Well… yeah… remember, I was trying to save face." He shifted and twitched slightly. "You see, it all depends on the point of view one sees it from, but the truth of the matter is I told them you broke my heart."

Like a baby bull, another snort blew out of me. "I'm listening, and oh boy, this better be good."

I desperately needed to understand how I was the instigator of the breakup which had devastated *me* to the core. There was no way a person would intentionally do that to themselves.

"Because of the dark place I was in and, believe me when I tell you it was dark, I told my family you had been the one to walk away from us."

My eyes widened. "Oh. My. Lanta. They think I left you over your disease?"

No wonder Bea hated me so much.

He waved his hands through the air and shook his head. "Oh no, no, no. Not at all. I told them you had broken up with me before I had even moved to Switzerland, and we were still communicating briefly, but you started dating some new guy and thought it was best to end what was left of us."

The way he scrunched his face with an *I'm-hoping-to-pull-this off* expression was not as adorable as he may have hoped.

"And they bought it?"

It was ridiculous to believe they'd fall for that. They were all highly intelligent, and I would've expected them to have seen right through the lie. They all knew how much I loved him, how madly in love I was, and how Carter was my sun, moon, and whole world.

A small smirk played on the fringes of his lips; it was neither jovial nor devious. "What can I say? I lied well."

"And a lot. Good grief. But Bea said *I* broke your heart, yet it was *you* who left me. Left us. How could I have broken your heart if you were the one handing out the damage? How could you have lied like that?" My tone grew more strength than expected.

The smirk wiped away with a swish of his hand, and his voice softened. "Leaving you was the hardest thing I ever did."

"You pushed me away. Your calls, your emails… they became… infrequent."

"Because I couldn't handle anything. And you, you were supposed to fight for me, to want to stay, but you didn't call as much, and your email communications drifted to nothing."

Oh, wow. My heart crashed into a brick wall. All this time, I figured he left me because school had become difficult and his studies were affected, or that he couldn't handle the lack of intimacy coming with a long-distance relationship. I had zero reason to believe it was because he was having a mental health crisis. Being thousands of miles away from all who loved him certainly didn't help either.

Carter continued as if I had pressed pause on the conversation to allow my brain to catch up. "I couldn't walk around pretending everything was all sunshine and roses, and I definitely didn't want to burden you with undue stress and emotional turmoil, considering I didn't even know how to deal with any of it myself." He sucked in and then released a slow breath. "I had to put the walls up, but in retrospect, it just seemed like you left so easily."

His gaze connected with my dumbfounded one.

My brain pressed fast forward to get to the part where my thoughts suddenly made sense. "How was I to have known what you were going through when you didn't share any of it with me? All that time, I worried it was our relationship, and how the long-distance thing was straining us because we needed to hold and touch the other. Figured we were slipping away, even if just for a bit until you came back home. I thought you believed in us – in me – to make it all work. That we'd get our happy ending." Tremors started in my chin, and my voice cracked as it fell. "I died the day you sent that email, an email…"

Shaking my head, a rush of emotions washed over me, making me relive that fateful moment as if it happened yesterday; the cut was so raw and so deep it very well could've happened twenty-four hours ago. My heart palpitated, my breath hitched, and an achiness tightened its stronghold on my chest.

"That was the worst day of my life until…" Dad passed away.

He hung his head. "I'm so sorry. It was selfish, but at the same time it was self-preservation."

Confusion, sadness, and some sort of empathy filled my bloodstream. With so many emotions swirling around, a rush of tears built up, blurring my vision. "After everything you've just shared, there's still something I don't understand."

"Yeah. Ask me anything." Softly spoken, he ran a finger under my eyes.

Worry caused me to cover my lips with my fingers, a preventative way to stop my emotions from bubbling out. Taking a deep breath, I dropped my hand to my lap and managed to blink the tears back in. "What does any of it have to do with the coffee plantation? If you were, pardon my language, so deep within yourself, why take a trip to a developing country?"

Rising, he tugged me into the living room, offering me a cozy and comfortable spot on the couch. I sat after he did.

"It was the weirdest thing. Now, I'm not known for flights of spontaneity,"

Hearing his statement made me lightly laugh. No, Carter was the total opposite; a planner to the core.

"There was a study being done out of one of

the universities there. A study between the correlation between caffeine and epilepsy, so I had to try to get some answers or find a cure or do something. All expenses were paid, and all throughout the study, I would receive top medical care, so it was a win-win." His face relaxed, and he leaned into the back of the couch. "Let me explain. Some researchers link high caffeine to more intense seizures, whereas there are some scientists who see some co-relation in people like me, that ironically, a higher caffeine intake seems to slow the rate a bit."

"A bit?"

"Remember how I said it was a genetic abnormality?"

So much information had been forthcoming, it was hard to remember all the details, but still, I indulged him.

"Something triggered on one of my chromosomes, or in, I forget which. But it happened deep within the DNA structure itself." His head tipped to the side. "Please don't ask me to explain it, as I'm still trying to figure it out myself."

"Fair enough." My head bobbed.

"Anyway, there are a few scientists and researchers who believe the higher ingestion of caffeine slows the rate of seizures. Enough that the anti-epileptic drugs were keeping things relatively balanced."

It was so much to unpack. I blinked rapidly and tried to understand everything he was saying. In my head, it was like a movie scene where graphs and vector images of chemical compounds floated past in a weird montage.

"And what happened?" I hated to think my presence in this small town had any effect on it. It just didn't make any sense.

"I'd met Diego, learned everything I needed to know about coffee bean production, and added the best puns into standard conversation. I learned with certain types of coffee beans, roasted in a particular way, they had a positive effect on me like a couple of researchers had predicted."

He tossed a quick glance into the kitchen. The bowl of chopped veggies still sat beside two untouched cups of brewed coffee.

"Until recently."

"Because?" I pushed closer, still trying to make sense of it all.

"A few months ago, I'd changed the way the beans were being roasted. Totally my fault." He blew out a puff of air which rattled the hair hanging over his forehead. "I figured I knew better than the researchers, but it turns out – surprise! – I don't understand my body well enough on a molecular level, and the change totally threw my system off. Like way off. I'm working on a new batch of roasted beans, and while the jury is still out, the way these beans are roasted, the theory is they should work alongside the medication instead of against it, like has happened lately." He reached across the table and produced a leather notebook, handing it to me.

It was thick and heavy, and after he gave me a quick nod, I rifled through it. The start of the book was June 1, and each page had a long, detailed list full of coffee bean jargon, the long medication names, times, foods he'd eaten, and how he felt emotionally. Each day was pages of material.

"As part of the ten-year study, I need to keep exceptional details of everything."

Ten years? That was a long time, and if he started... I closed the book which felt like a personal diary rather than a list of day-to-day activities. "So you're close to the end of the study?"

"Oh yeah, I hope so, but I might keep adding to it. If I can find the right balance, it could help people with the genetic abnormality like I have, which I understand is a pretty small group, a percent of a percent kind of thing. But if I can help just one other person…"

That was the Carter I loved. Always willing to help another out. Even at great personal sacrifice.

My back pushed into the sofa. "Isn't caffeine a chemical or something? Wouldn't a stimulator work against someone with a sensitivity to chemicals, or whatever it is that causes a seizure." Sheesh, there was so much I needed to learn.

"I don't fully understand the deep level of how the brain works and regulates everything and why what works on someone else doesn't work on me, but I do know after some genetic testing, there's a marker on one of my genes, or something like that, which wears down the way my body responds to the drugs, so after a while, there'll be nothing chemical to help me, at least not as it stands now, and I'll need to find other natural ways to deal with my disease, if it, you know doesn't…" He shrugged, but this time I did know.

If the disease didn't kill him first. What a lot of pressure to weigh on a person.

"And the coffee helps?"

He grimaced. "Ironic, isn't it, especially considering Dr. Moins in Biology class warned of the dangers of caffeine."

And other stimulants, which were neither here nor there.

"But keeping a healthy diet free of sugar also seems to help." He faced me. "It's all about balance. A very delicate balance."

I reflected and didn't remember ever seeing him eat a donut or add sweeteners to his drinks. "And that aids in keeping you…?" I didn't want to say healthy as it implied he was unhealthy, and maybe he was clinically, but…

Ugh, I wanted to scream about the whole thing but suddenly, I was starting to understand why he pushed me away – why it was necessary to break *my* heart. In a way, in his dark and twistedly warped way, he was protecting me from the new life he was now living.

Just thinking about all the ramifications, my heart broke all over again, but in ways I didn't fully comprehend.

"Oh, Carter." I climbed over and snuggled into his arms as the tears started streaming once more, but I didn't care. I stared deeply into his eyes, searching for the love we once shared. Daring it to release itself from the darkness. "I wished you'd been upfront with me and told me everything. I would've been here for you." I paused to catch my breath. "With you, I was always all in."

"Now you know everything." He kissed the top of my head, and I melted into his arms.

"And I'm never leaving."

"You say that now, but when the going gets tough, you'll be gone. They all leave at some point."

There was such a venom to his words that I had to shake out of his embrace and stare the man down. Then another conversation hit me. "That's why she left you, isn't it?"

He didn't meet my gaze and got up off the couch, walking into the kitchen with a purpose. The eggs took the full onslaught of his sudden burst of anger as he cracked them one by one on the edge of the counter.

Jumping off the couch, I ran to wrap my arms around him. Everything I wanted to say sounded so wrong, and I didn't have the foggiest of ideas on what to do. Rather than think it through, I did what I knew to do best; I let my instincts guide me.

I spun him around, searching out the suddenly haunted gaze clouding his eyes, and allowed him access to my heart – the one he'd always had. Feeling free, I cupped his face, stroking his soft beard.

"Carter, you listen to me. I'm here, and I'm not leaving. Not now, not ever. If you're going to walk a dark path, then I'll walk it beside you, tethering you to my soul. And if you need to sing in the sunshine, I'll cheer you on. You may have fooled me once, but not anymore."

In one fell swoop, he lifted me onto the counter and braced his hands on my waist, his gaze searching the depths of my eyes.

"It's okay." I tried a light smile with a friendly tone. "You can kiss me. We've waited long enough."

There was no hesitation this time and he pressed his perfect lips against mine while my body simultaneously sent waves of electricity pulsing through to my extremities. In a flash, the ocean between us dried up and we were picking up right where we left off.

I held back, waiting to feel his kiss. To feel him kissing me first. When his lips touched mine, and he took control, I surrendered. Fully and without reservation. My fingers threaded through his thick hair, I pulled him close and begged him not to leave me – he needed to know everything would be okay. For the first time in years, I was connected to another living soul on a deep and meaningful level, and I allowed that rush to guide me as time melted away.

I clung to him as if he was my lifeline when it very well could've been the other way around.

Chapter Fifteen

THE REST OF the week zoomed on by, and Friday night's workshop went off without a hitch. Instead of retreating into a nervous wreck who weakly announced the directions of the activity, my inner entertainer pushed to the surface and ran the show. I was excited – energetic – and found myself enjoying the teaching aspect. Who knew?

Stanley pulled me aside after the last group exited.

"Well done. You rocked the workshop like a champ, I barely even needed to be in here." He gave me a small wink as he untied his apron and stood in the doorframe between the two stores.

I grabbed the broom, rather pleased myself with how the night went. Everything had been set up well in advance, and all the attendees raved about their trees. An added bonus, at least for me, was how the whole place smelled like Christmas, and combined with the music playing, the magic of the season had descended upon Daisy and Dahlia's. It was wonderful and infectious. I'd finally found something which made me feel accomplished and useful, and it was not what I'd expected.

I stopped sweeping. "Hey, Stanley."

"Yeah." He stepped back into the space.

"This room, this store. What was it before?"

The space was huge, at least double the size of Daisy and Dahlia's, maybe even triple.

"It was a boutique of some sort. Never visited it really, kinda girlie, but Daisy did. Liked all the makeup and hair things." He lifted a shoulder.

"And it gets rented out?"

"Occasionally. The owners don't want to sell, but periodically they'll lease the space out. I get lucky and get rental time in late November, early December."

The way he said it put my train of thought back on the tracks. "How long has it been empty?"

He gave his chin a solid rub. "Gosh, two, maybe three years?"

"Where did you run the workshops before?" As

there was no way there was room in the flower shop.

"Use to run it out of Carl's place up on Mountain Lane. He'd rent us the space on the main floor to use on condition the customers also ordered something. It was one-night mid-week, not the five we run now, but it was pricey. Oh, boy. One night there was two-thirds the cost of the full week here, so I reached out to Lexington, that's the owners of this place," he waved his hand around the workshop space, "and inquired. The rest they say is history."

"And he or she holds onto the space for years? Seems like bad business, especially if they can't sell."

"For some, I s'pose but whatever. Ain't my business because I get a monster of a deal when I need it."

"I'll bet." I glanced around the space, taking it in, and imagining bigger and better ideas.

It was huge, and if a boutique was here, they had to have had a lot of products on display. I could imagine walls lined with tubes of lipstick, blush, mascara, and all the pretty things.

Like a bolt of lightning, I suddenly saw the space filled with hardware items like my dad sold, with a table in the middle for customers to work on small projects. Dad had always enjoyed helping a neighbour construct a birdhouse or having a few kids make their own toolboxes or tic-tac-toe games. Helping with those had been interesting, and a deep well of nostalgia filled me as I recalled all the fun we used to have. Working in the hardware store hadn't been work for Dad, it was a passion. And reviewing tonight's workshop, I had channelled that passion too. Suddenly the job wasn't work; it was fun.

The rental space was roughly the same size as Gallagher's, maybe a hair bigger, but Dad's shop had also been in a bigger city, so if he hadn't carried something, someone else did.

Was seeing this workshop space in a new light a sign of some sort? In a long list of impulsive things, leasing or renting or buying this space would be one of the most spontaneous things I've ever done. But could it be fun? Could I make it work?

It would be hard getting it all started, but I wasn't beneath putting in the hours - if that's what I truly wanted. The money was there, waiting for just the right thing, that's what I'd promised Dad. For now, though, it was a thought, and before I let the idea run away, I needed to let it percolate a bit.

THE MOST HANDSOME angel to ever walk on the Earth knocked on my motel door at precisely five-thirty the next evening.

Steeling my breath, I opened the non-creaking door and invited him in.

"Hey, brew-tiful."

It never failed to send a rush of warmth throughout my body at hearing him call *me* gorgeous.

"I love what you've done with the place. The door doesn't squeak." Glancing around with a solid nod he took off his toque and stuffed it into his pocket. "And… I see you tidied this time."

"*This time* I was actually expecting company."

He stared over my shoulder and stalked to the kitchen sink. "No way! You weren't kidding when you said you still had this."

"Did you think I lied?"

He admired the mug, giving it a solid once over before he set it down on top of a stack of newspapers. "Nah, it's not in you." After staring at it for a few heartbeats, he wrapped his arms around my waist and tucked me perfectly into his arms. "Are you ready for tonight?"

"Since I have no idea what to expect, my expectations are low."

"Oh?" He raised a brow.

"Then everything that happens will be perfect and magical."

"Well, now you're really raising the bar." A light laugh made his eyes twinkle. "Perfect and magical aren't two words normally associated with my dates."

"They are when I look back upon ours." I wasn't prepared for the sweet expression growing full strength, but seeing it made my insides all tingly yet powerful. "And... besides, Nina said that's where she met her true love."

"You think you'll meet your true love there?"

I shrugged and grinned, tipping my chin down. "Maybe, but I think I've already met him."

Staring into my eyes, he asked, "Before I forget, how is it you know more about my employee than I do?"

I looked into his charming face, glancing at the fringe of blond hair peeking out from under his toque. "What can I say? Maybe she feels comfortable with me since I'm not her boss. Or, maybe, she wanted to sell me on the idea of going."

"Do you need a lot of convincing to attend this tree lighting?"

"Is there anything you can do which would

result in me not checking it out?" I raised myself onto the balls of my feet and gave my lips a quick lick.

Carter took the bait and leaned down to plant his lips upon mine, pressing with the gentlest of pushes, and took command of the situation.

The kiss lit me on fire as the embers deep in my soul sparked to life. It felt great to feel so alive again. Threading my fingers under his hat and through his thick and messy hair, I pulled in close and opened my heart to him.

After a throaty and low sigh, he separated from me as the heat spread to taint his cheeks.

I cleared my throat. "If you keep kissing me like that, there won't be a tree lighting ceremony to go to, and you promised me a lot of fun activities."

"I'm making up for lost time." He tipped his forehead against mine.

"We'll get there. Promise."

"Fine." He mock-whined. "Don your warmest winter gear. Let me grab your jacket."

As I put on my thick white boots with a solid grip, he grabbed my jacket off the back of the chair.

"I still can't believe you have this." He lifted the mug once more, and this time, narrowed his eyes slightly as he stared at the papers underneath.

Dang. Dang. Dang.

In a heartbeat and with an easy swipe, I grabbed the newspaper and folded it in half, tossing it into the trash.

"What was that?" A serious expression swooped over his face.

"On my way home from Daisy and Dahlia's, I grabbed one of those archaic things they called a newspaper, and just started looking at different job ads." Yes, it was all a lie, but I just wasn't ready to tell him I was searching for a new place. It seemed so rushed, and in a month of spontaneous events, I wanted to make sure I was doing the right thing.

"I thought you were happy with Stanley?"

"Oh, I am." I kicked at a black fluffy part which had escaped from my thick socks. Bending down, I snatched it off the floor and rolled it into a ball before adding it to the garbage. "And I'm beyond grateful for the opportunity Stanley has given me, I'm just... well, I'm keeping my options open."

The tight-knit expression told me all I needed to know – he wasn't buying my story. He had seen what was circled.

"If you say so." He brushed the hair off my cheeks before planting a tender, teasing kiss on my aching lips. "We should get going."

"Right now?" I whined.

"There's so much to do, we'll barely be able to squeeze it all in before the tree lighting ceremony."

"Well, I can't wait to see what this is all about. Lead the way." I donned my toque with two pom-poms and pulled on a thick pair of mittens.

Hand in hand, we walked from the motel over to a field full of roaming bodies. From the looks of things, I would've guessed half the town was already there.

"Do you want to go skating first?" He gently tugged me toward the skate shack which sat at the end of the ice. Strings of lights stretched out from it to points across the frozen water.

After a glance to the surface, I noticed a lack of sideboards and shook my head. "Uh… I haven't skated in years, so probably not. I'll fall too much."

The idea of a bruised butt didn't sit too well with me.

"Then I'll catch you lots, and we don't have to go fast. Plus, it's a great way to hold hands and be all romantic. I mean, just look at the surroundings."

"Wow, when you commit to something, you really go all in, don't you?" I giggled as I spoke, but I took his words to heart and scanned the area, trying to see it as he did.

Beyond the skate shack, stood a dark and lone tree, taller than any I'd ever seen before; it would put the one in New York City to shame. Beyond that, almost surrounding it in a semi-circle, were trees half the size of the big one, all decorated with coloured lights. A group of carollers dressed in matching robes stood singing near the skate shack, and three food trucks were parked near the huge bonfire surrounded by hay bales.

He reached for my hand. "Ever since the moment your credit card wouldn't work, I've wanted to hold your hand, and I don't intend on letting go."

"Since then? Wow. That's a long time to hold out."

"Some things are worth waiting for."

"And sometimes," I said, cocking my eyebrow, "all that's needed is a grocery worker intent on showing off at precisely the right moment to give a little push toward the goal."

Carter didn't look impressed. "Or that." He tugged me toward the ice rink. "Let's not talk about him, okay?"

We stopped in front of the skate shack and gave our skate sizes to the guy, and then silently meandered over to the hay bales edging the ice.

It had been years since I'd slipped on skates, and I'd forgotten how much I hated tying the laces and tightening the boot way up past my ankle. Why couldn't they make skates easier to put on?

"Let me do this for you." He grabbed my left foot, and tugged the laces into compliance, doing the same with the right until they were both snug but not tight.

Whereas Carter popped up onto his skates, I slowly rose and wobbled like a newborn deer. Then came the horrible attempt at moving on the slick surface. He skated; I shuffled like a toddler on skates for the first time. However, as the old adage goes, it was like riding a bike and after a bit, I finally got the hang of it, sort of, at least I was able to step glide and not skitter around.

Effortlessly, he skated backward while keeping his hands just near enough to reach out to grab me if I fell. It turned out, I was more stable without holding his hand. And as much as I didn't want to, I worried what would happen if *he* fell, which was the exact thing he had worried about in sharing his diagnosis. Would a fall, or a bump to the head, cause him to have a seizure? However, watching him become an extension of the ice took my mind off worrying. As far as skating went, he was more

Canadian than I was.

But twenty minutes on the blades of torture was enough to wear me out physically and send a deep ache through muscles I didn't know existed. However, I was now warm, and sweaty, for an entirely different reason.

"Want to sit around the fire?" I asked, falling with a solid thump onto the unforgiving hay bale. My aching tailbone was going to berate me for hours after that.

"That idea has a whole latte potential."

I wanted to throw a pun back in his direction, but he used the word I had prepped for just the right moment. Scrolling through my brain, I conjured up another word. "You mocha me laugh."

With a giant smile, he fell beside me untying his skates and setting them off to the side after slipping his boots back on.

Freeing my hands from the warmth of my mittens, I started loosening the laces, wondering how long it would take before I lost feeling in my fingertips. It was cold enough my breath created giant puffs of white, breezy clouds.

"Please, allow me." Before I could go any further, he propped my foot onto his lap and untied the laces, tugging and pulling which allowed cold air to strangle my ankle.

I shivered uncontrollably.

"You're freezing."

"That's why I want to sit around the fire."

"Only the second-best activity here."

I leaned back onto my palms. "You're really hyping up this whole tree lighting thing. It can't be that amazing, can it?"

"You'll see."

Under the glow from the overhead string lights, it wasn't hard to miss the building twinkle in his eyes, the one I'd always been drawn to in my younger years. It was sweet to see it slowly returning.

He gave the underside of my foot a gentle massage when it was free of the skate, and until he touched me there, I didn't know that part of my foot ached so much.

I groaned and lightly closed my eyes to the rolling sensation against the balls of my feet and into the arch. "Oh, my, that feels heavenly."

"Easy there." His head was tipped down, but he turned to look at me through his left eye.

Reaching over my lap, he grabbed my boot and after another amazing massage, slipped it overtop my foot.

I set my foot down and instantly propped up the other.

"So presumptuous, aren't we?"

"You're not getting away with only one foot rub. What would the other foot say? She'd be all jealous and may be liable to kick you out of spite or something."

"Well, we can't have that now, can we?"

Like an expert, his thumbs massaged right into the sore spots and released a satisfying sound as a weird sort of heat blanketed my toes. It was sweet bliss and felt like the weight of the world had been released. I'd never been one to love a foot rub, and most of the time protested my feet even being touched, but with his magical hands digging into all the sweet spots, it was intensely pleasurable.

"All better?" Carter set my foot down; he could've rubbed my feet all night long with no complaints from me.

"Much, thank you." I stood and pulled him onto his feet.

He hopped up with a jump and landed directly in front of me, staring down beneath his beautiful, full lashes. His lips parted slightly, allowing a puff of white air to escape.

Snowflakes started falling around us, and not

just the tiny, wet variety. These were huge, big enough to contain all of Whoville. As the snow fell, the air around us fell silent, and a huge snowflake landed on Carter's lashes, bobbing up and down with each blink.

Tenderly, I brushed it onto my mitten and held it in front of him. "Make a wish."

"You're supposed to do that with eyelashes, silly, not snowflakes." His gaze fell to the mitten. "And it's melted already."

"Well, that's promising." My voice fell.

"It is, actually. Maybe all my dreams have come true, and the snowflake knew it to be true."

"Oh, Carter. You do say the sweetest things."

"Of course, I do. You seem to have the power to bring them out of me." He gave me a wink and tugged on my arm. "Now let's go see Nina about getting you a new brew so you can warm up."

BESIDE THE PARKED food trucks was the Coffee Loft Cabin. Not so much a food truck as a permanent setup in a small sea-can with the logo beside a pop-up window.

"Is this here all the time?"

"Of course. Everyone needs a hot chocolate

after skating. The two go hand in hand."

We walked over to the back of the cabin, where he punched in a code and unlocked the door.

"You can warm up inside."

"What? No way." I didn't want to get underfoot. There was a long line up out front and no doubt, Nina was going to be hopping.

"It's a perk of being the manager." He waved me in.

"Oh hey, you two." Nina stopped brewing and gave us both the once over, nodding happily as she grabbed a couple of paper cups.

Carter scanned the area. "How's it *bean* tonight?"

"A whole latte crazy fun."

I rolled my eyes while stifling a laugh. "Are coffee puns part of the training?"

He snapped his finger. "Nope, but they really should be. I'll have Bea update the manuals."

Nina hip-checked me as she lidded the cups. "His puns tend to rub off on me, and it becomes part of the lingo." She turned to the window and passed out the two drinks with a genuine smile. "Java nice night, mkay?"

Carter fussed around the tiny space. "What would you like?"

"What are my options? I can't imagine you'd have a whole store here?" Although, seeing all the machines, it was a strong possibility.

From the top shelf, he grabbed a small silver bag, and using a stylish measuring spoon, he filled two pods with ground beans. "If I may, I'd been doing some more research and trial tastings, and think this might be a hit. If not for me, definitely for the coffee lovers."

"Oooh, colour me intrigued. I want whatever it is you're brewing."

The machine hissed and steamed and dribbled its dark roast into the paper cup.

After a minute, he handed it to me and made himself one. "It's tall, dark, and handsome."

"Like you," I added quickly.

A shy grin spread from cheek to cheek. "Add whatever you need to it. Fridge is over there."

"I like it this way."

Our gaze connected and held until a long, languishing hiss ended his coffee brew. Coffee capped and sleeves slipped on, we exited with a quick wave to Nina and perused the food truck offerings, deciding on Italian for supper.

Finishing up our delicious food, Carter cleared his throat. "So, I know we are new to this relationship – sort of – and you are wanting to take it slow, but I'm wondering if…"

Emotionless, he just sat there, letting the glow of the bonfire dance across his face. There was no change to his expression, and no words forthcoming, both of which worried me slightly.

"What?" I finally asked when he still hadn't spoken.

He took a long sip of his special blend. If it was anything like mine, it was likely lukewarm at best. The paper cups didn't do much to retain heat, not when it was cold and snowy.

"Do you, or would you, join Bea and me for supper on Wednesday?" Even under the cover of his scarf, the bobbing Adam's Apple was undeniable.

A light snort rolled out of me, and I set my fork across my empty plate. The food truck had made the best ravioli, and in the most unladylike way, I had inhaled my food.

"That's a big ask."

"It's just my sister and her boyfriend, and me. Nothing major..."

"She hates me, remember? Thinks I broke your heart."

"I'll set her straight."

"You mean, you haven't yet?" I perched

forward on my haybale, making myself as physically uncomfortable as I was emotionally.

I just wasn't sure about being in such a restrictive environment with his sister. We'd never gotten along, and after Carter's big lie, it just wasn't high on my wish list of things to do.

"Don't you worry. I'll tell her it was all on me."

My eyes widened. "When? Before or after we're married?"

The glow from the flickering flames danced across the building smirk. "Wow. Already thinking about marriage?"

"Just answer. When are you going to tell her?"

"Before Wednesday. I promise." He held up his pinkie.

I linked mine with his. "You know I don't take lightly to promises."

"Yeah, I know."

"So you'll tell her?"

"Yes."

"And if you don't?" I needed a backup plan, something to hold against him in the event of him baling and not telling the truth.

He inhaled and took another sip of his drink, tipping it back to empty the cup completely. "How about... If I don't tell her, you can punch me."

"Why would I ever punch you? I hate violence. Wait…" I narrowed my eyes. "That's just your way of getting out of it. You need to do better than that."

"Fine. If I don't tell her, I'll warm your car and sweep the snow off it for a week."

"I start the car from an app."

"But it's supposed to snow all week." He wore a hopeful expression.

"I need more than that."

"And… I'll shovel the walkway in front of Daisy and Dahlia's."

"That benefits Stanley more than me."

"Not if you're working that day." Even under the hanging strands of string lights, the twinkle in his eyes outshone the brightest bulbs.

"Yeah, that's acceptable." It wasn't the best bet, but it would do. Whatever it took to get that sparkle to stay put.

In agreeance, I shook his hand, thinking how nice it could be to have someone sweep the snow off my car. Back home, I parked underground so it was never an issue.

Begrudgingly though, I sighed. "Then I'll come. What can I bring?"

He laughed in relief. "I've seen your kitchen; you don't need to bring anything."

"That's not happening. Put me down for dessert." Carter went to open his mouth. "I'll find something amazing; you'll see." I squeezed his hand and took a sip of my now iced coffee. As I drank the last of it, the flavour hit me. "Is there some kind of chocolate in this?"

"It's negligible, but yes."

It was an after-taste, but it was like a dark chocolate, the kind with the barest hint of sweetness to it. "You know, you should have a good mocha recipe for the Coffee Loft."

"Something with a spicy kick?"

It was as if he read my mind. "Yes, like a cinnamon or something."

"I'm working on something similar as a new release launch for February. In time for Valentine's Day."

"Ooh, tell me more."

"Later." He winked. "I'm keeping it under wraps for now."

"You won't even tell me, your girlfriend?"

"I like the sound of that."

Was he blushing?

No one to skip a beat though, he carried on, "Are you going to tell me about those circled ads on your table?" He cocked an eyebrow with enough strength to push up the brim of his toque.

Jeepers creepers, he had seen them, and I had hoped he hadn't. My last apartment, the one I was still paying for but not living in, my dad had helped with all the finer details and asked all the right questions. This time, I needed to do it on my own, to prove I was a capable grown-up.

A rocket fired into the sky with a loud boom, and I screamed.

"Oh, great," Carter jumped to his feet and gathered our garbage from the food trucks. The toasted ravioli was delicious. "The show's about to begin."

"That's how they warn about the tree lighting?" I handed him my paper plate, adding my empty coffee cup on top.

"Of course, come on. I have the most perfect spot for us." He dragged me past the food trucks, around the skating rink, and halfway across the field until we stopped under a tall tree – the kind of tree that in the summer would be fabulously full of leaves and shade a great area – maybe even make for a cozy picnic spot with a blanket.

Once under the naked tree branches, I pressed my back against the sturdy trunk and watched the snowflakes continue to dance to the ground.

Carter stepped closer and tugged on the neck of my jacket, wrapping it tighter over me. "You're going to catch a cold if you don't stay warm."

I laughed but appreciated the gesture. "I can't catch a virus just standing outside exposed, I have to be within the vicinity of someone who is sick."

"That may be true but keeping warm will help."

"And you're going to keep me warm?" Sure, it was ripe with wanton desire, but kissing Carter had been one of my favourite activities.

He pulled my toque down over the tips of my ears. "I can try."

With a tip of his head towards mine, his heated lips brushed against mine, igniting an instant fire deep in my soul. The longer he stayed attached, the more the snowflakes were going to puddle on my jacket and hat. Carter's kisses were incredible, but to feel them bring me back to life, that was magical.

He broke us apart. "I sure do love kissing you."

"As do I."

Somewhere, far off in the distance, a countdown began from ten, and it forced my gaze away from him over to the giant tree in the distance.

Feeling flushed with a radiant heat, I twisted

slightly away from Carter. "The tree lighting?"

He stepped behind me and dropped his chin onto my shoulder. His breathy voice tickled my ears. "Just watch."

As the crowd chanted down to zero, the giant tree lit from the bottom up in a slow, dazzling display of twinkling, coloured lights. As the star on the top lit up, fireworks launched into the sky.

The first blast propelled me backward into the manly wall of Carter, and he snuggled tighter to me.

"I should've warned you about the fireworks, but I wanted it to be a surprise."

"Oh, it's a surprise all right." And one I couldn't tear my gaze away from.

Watching – and then feeling – each mini-explosion set my senses on overload in a way I was starting to crave. I wanted more, and needed more, and spending time with Carter was absolutely everything I craved within my soul.

I couldn't wait to move here permanently and start a business, but I had to wait until the ink was dry to say anything since bad luck followed me like a lost puppy.

I turned to Carter and tipped my head up, exposing my neck to the biting cold. Flash by dazzling flash, I watched the fireworks in his gaze until I closed my eyes and pressed into him for a kiss that rivaled the most colourful and explosive fireworks.

Chapter Sixteen

THE CALL KEPT ringing until just before it went to voicemail, a breathless voice answered. "Hello?"

"Amanda?" It sure didn't sound like her, and I double-checked I had called her number.

"Yeah, it's me. Sorry, I just finished a workout."

I triple-checked the time. It was two in the afternoon – a weird time of the day for a … Oh, the lightbulb went off.

"I'll call you back."

"It's all good. I've got a moment. Silas just started making a late lunch. What's up?"

"You just claimed first dibs with that comment. Silas?"

Her breezy sigh crossed the phone line. "Yeah.

New beau. Broke up with Kevin at that new place over on the east end. I just couldn't be with him anymore. It was so blah. Even the breakup was boring. He simply shrugged and said he was cool with it before he got up, shook my hand, and stuck me with the bill. Can you believe that?"

I laughed out loud. She sounded more upset about having to pay the bill than anything else. "Had you ordered yet?"

"Nah, just had drinks."

"So it wasn't that big a deal then."

"Big enough."

I drew circles on my notepad as she whined. "So then, who's Silas?"

"So get this." Her voice jumped half an octave. "As I'm sitting there feeling all weirded out over the bizarre nature of the breakup, I watched as this other guy got dumped by his girlfriend. She tossed her water glass at him. Feeling bad, I handed him my napkin and said *tough night for couples, eh?* and he started laughing. Next thing I know the two of us are sharing a tray of nachos and a bottle of chianti."

"That's a super weird combo."

"That's what I said." The mock surprise was ripe on the tip of her tongue. "And that's what Silas said too, but you know what, it was perfect. We stayed for the whole evening until the server told us it was time for them to close down. Cara, I shut down a restaurant."

"That's a first." A bar, nope, she'd done that several times over, but a restaurant, that had to be a new one.

"The next day, we met after work, and we talked all night long again. He's so funny and personable and just unlike any guy I've dated before. He's just so..." Her voice faded away.

"Perfect?"

"Not even close." I could also picture her shaking her head and waving a hand through the air. "He hates cats and dogs, and he loves country music. Blech." Two of Amanda's pet peeves.

She was a cat person, through and through, and if not for all her allergies, no doubt there would be a dozen pets in her place. But country music? That was usually a hard pass on any guy. This one clearly had something special to offer.

"When are you going out again?"

"Well, he's here. Actually, I'm at his place. He lives a few blocks from the law court building."

That was a pretty nice part of Red Deer, with ample trails and parks and the winding Red Deer river just footsteps away.

"We've seen each other every day after work since we had our mutual breakups. He's so easy to talk to, and we get along so well. It feels like we've known each other forever."

I couldn't stop the smile from spreading across my face. "Amanda, I am truly happy for you. You sound so over the moon."

"You have no idea. Or…" She paused. "Maybe you do?"

"Well, I'm not madly in love," or in lust, like I was thinking was a true possibility with Amanda. "But Carter and I have talked and really worked things out. We're officially seeing each other again."

"Why do I hear hesitation in your voice?"

"There's none of that. We're both all in. He's, well… he's," but I couldn't say it. I didn't think it was my place to blurt out his condition, not even to my best friend. "We're working on resolving our past demons, so it means we're erring on the side of caution."

She laughed. "That's a first for you. How slow are you talking here?"

"Slow and swoony, like a fresh start but better because we know each other. We had a great heart-to-heart on Thursday morning, and last night we went to this Tree Lighting Ceremony in the park."

"And after all that romantic fun, then what?" Was she perched on the edge of her seat waiting for hot and sweaty details that never happened?

"No." It hadn't even been a thought that crossed our minds, well, maybe not his because he'd been a perfect gentleman. "We laid together on the couch and watched two old episodes of Grey's Anatomy, but mostly, we talked. We're catching up on a lot of things. We're in a good place right now."

"Oh wow. You are taking it slow with just talking. But why?"

"There's a lot on his plate, and there's a lot on mine."

"Yeah right, like what?"

"I'm working at the flower shop and, Stanley put me in charge of running their Grinch Tree workshop."

He'd even asked at work if it was okay to run two more workshops early next week since there was a high demand.

"Shut up, you are not."

"Yeah. And the best part is, Amanda, I really am enjoying it. I loved teaching the class. I loved getting my hands involved. My boss, Stanley, he's this old soul type who tells it like it is, but yet is gentle and kind. Reminds me of Dad a little." A lot when I really thought about it. "All around, it's just a great work atmosphere. Probably one of the best jobs I've had in the last few years."

"Who are you and where is my best friend, the one who hates getting her hands dirty and would rather type than talk to people? This whole quarter-life crisis of yours is interesting."

"I'm still here, just finding myself. Maybe it is a quarter-life crisis, but I'm loving the change and Ridge Heights. The people are awesome. This town is fun, and the ceremony last night, put anything you and I have enjoyed to shame. We went skating and had this amazing new coffee and the best ravioli around the bonfire."

"Wow. I'm shocked, truth be told. Figured this move of yours was one of your spontaneous acts of grandeur, where you run off to find the next best thing. I have to admit, I'm impressed."

"Maybe getting fired and dumped was a blessing in disguise as I found this place totally accidentally, and it's been…"

"What?"

"Never mind. It'll sound stupid and cliché."

"Try me."

I sighed, and even though she couldn't see my

face, I tipped my head down. "It's like I didn't know how much I needed this place when I didn't even know it existed."

There was nothing from her end of the line.

"Amanda?"

"You sound happy, Cara. Honestly."

"Really? You're not just saying that?"

"I know I've only known you for a few years, but in all those years, you've never sounded so lit up, so full of life. Maybe this town, this Ridge Heights, is the place for you to be, and maybe part of that is Carter."

My smile grew into a mega-watt grin. "He's fantastically awesome. You'd like him."

"So, you're staying a wee bit longer than you'd planned?"

I held my breath and rolled my bottom lip between my teeth. "Yeah. Actually, I'm looking into buying or renting, or leasing, or a combination of two."

"Wait, what? Walk me through all of that."

I explained about the vacant space beside the flower shop, and then added in how I found myself daydreaming about finding the perfect home.

"You want to sell your apartment here?"

"Considering it, yes." The words rolled out too

easily, so there was a lot of truth within. "I am touring a couple of places on Tuesday. Nothing big or fancy, but yeah."

"Okay, that sounds like the impulsive Cara I know, but even she wouldn't just list her place and up and move."

"But I did half of that very thing. You helped me pack."

"Because I thought you'd spend time with Carter and get the closure I felt you needed about the whole breakup. Her voice pitched, and I no longer heard the enthusiasm and excitement. Instead, it was confusion muddled with hurt and disbelief. "I didn't honestly think you'd consider moving there permanently and buying a place to turn into a hardware store."

"Well, I am staying here, and the more I think about opening the shop, the better I feel inside. I'm not nearly as worried about this as I was trying to find another failed marketing position. It's almost like—"

"Don't you dare say it's a sign."

My shoulders slumped. "You really need to come and see it here. Maybe you'll change your mind about it all."

She sighed. "Maybe I should. I'm starting to

get concerned."

"Because you love me? And you want the best for me? Just like I do with, and for, you."

"Yeah. Something like that."

"I love you, Amanda."

"I love you too." There was a slight pause. "Should I assume you're busy at Christmas?"

"I hadn't even thought about it yet."

It was less than three weeks away – it should've been more on my mind than it was, but with Carter, the house viewings, and reading the details on the leasing of the building next to Stanley's place, there was just so much to think about.

"Tell you what, to make this easy, let's do a Boxing Day get-together. Rather than fight the crowds for deals on things I probably don't need, why don't Silas and I drive there, and we'll have lunch. I'll meet your guy, you meet mine."

"Sounds like the perfect plan."

"Or maybe I should show up earlier than that. I'm really borderline concerned."

"I'm fine. Better than fine. You'll see."

Now to make it a self-fulling prophecy.

Chapter Seventeen

AT MY MOTEL on the fateful Wednesday evening, Carter lowered himself into Casper and we started heading toward his sister's. Frantically, he patted his pockets. "Oh, beans. I forgot something at the Coffee Loft. It's on my desk. Do you mind?"

I took the next turn back toward the coffee shop, where I found a vacant spot nearer to his place.

"Can you give me a couple minutes? I'll be right back."

"Sure thing."

"Thanks." He placed a quick kiss upon my cheek before exiting the car.

"Wait, I'll come with you."

Hand in hand we walked down the street and I

paused at the base of the stairs, my gaze focused on a couple heading in our direction.

"Everything okay?" Carter asked as he tugged my hand.

"Amanda?" I called out, releasing my grip and running to meet my best friend with a giant hug. "What are you doing here?"

She shrugged. "I couldn't wait until Boxing Day. I wanted to surprise you."

"I'm so surprised. So pleasantly surprised." My gaze meandered over to the gentleman beside her. "You must be Silas?"

The tall blond, who was totally not Amanda's typical type, extended his hand. "Cara, an absolute pleasure to meet you in person. I've heard so much about you."

"Oh gosh. All good I hope." I raised a curious eyebrow at my friend.

He wrapped an arm around her shoulders and squeezed. "Don't worry, she's never mentioned your quarter-life crisis."

"Thanks a lot." I playfully smacked Amanda as I laughed, stepping back into the hard wall of my boyfriend. "I'm so sorry. Carter, this is—"

"Amanda and Silas."

Amanda beamed. "You're the coffee guy.

Cara's first love. It's an absolute pleasure."

I should've been embarrassed, but it wasn't happening. Instead, pressing into Carter a little more, I asked, "Why didn't you call me and tell me you were coming?"

"Part of the surprise. I went to the motel room but there was no answer. Searching out, I found that flower shop, but the old man there said you were finished for the day and suggested I try the Coffee Loft. So here I am. I took a small tour of this town and I'm impressed. I can certainly see the appeal."

She pointed to the trees and window storefronts all wrapped in white lights. The mountains were prominently on display under the waning glow of the moon.

"So, where's a great place to get dinner?"

"Ah, well... We already have plans with Carter's sister. We were on our way there, but he needed to make a stop here first."

"Speaking of which, give me a quick minute. Excuse me." Without further warning, he jumped up the stairs and entered the Coffee Loft.

Amanda narrowed her eyes and tipped her head.

"He does that." However, I wasn't going to apologize for it. I knew he'd return and jump back in like he hadn't just vanished before our eyes. "So, I'm really sorry I can't make dinner."

And I really wanted to go too. Hanging out with Bea wasn't high on my list of things to do but hanging out with Amanda and seeing her and Silas together? That would be fun.

Amanda nudged Silas. "Told you we should've called first."

"Really? *You* said this would be more fun." He kissed the side of her cheek. "But that's okay, I'll be the fall guy." Silas turned to me. "Next time, I promise I'll give you a heads up." A wink followed.

How cute were these two together?

She shrugged. "It's no biggie." Although her fallen expression said it was. "So, where's a good place to eat? I didn't see any fast-food joints."

"There's only a couple, right at the turn-off into town. By the gas station."

"Oh." Her waxing disappointment hung on.

Feeling two feet tall because she'd made the trek out to the mountains to see me and I wasn't even available, I caved. "I'll cancel dinner. Carter can go without me."

"Nah. I wouldn't do that to you. You had plans."

"It's okay. Carter will understand."

"What will I understand?" He appeared by my side.

"That I'm cancelling plans for dinner. Go without me. Take the dessert."

"Won't be necessary."

"What?" I looked up at his handsome face. "Bea loves extra company and honestly won't have an issue."

Facing Amanda with an unsure expression, I shrugged. "What do you think? And you don't have to. I can cancel on her."

A mischievous expression filled her face and she leaned into Silas. "Carter that's awfully sweet of you, I'd love to accept. Silas?"

He nodded. "Of course. Where can we stop and pick up a fine bottle of red?"

Directions were handed out and we took off in separate directions as worry and apprehension filled my soul.

As I parked outside Bea's house, a nice-sized bungalow tucked toward the edge of town with a decent view of downtown Ridge Heights, a heavy weight descended upon my shoulders.

"You'll be fine. Plus, you'll have Amanda here." Carter rubbed my thigh, but I still wasn't convinced.

"Maybe. I just need to gather myself, pray for peace, and ready for the possibility of some harsh words."

He closed his eyes and pinched the bridge of his nose.

"Are you okay?" Although he had stated he didn't want me to monitor his every move, I couldn't help myself.

Since he'd arrived at my motel room, where I was finishing the sugar-free cinnamon coffee cake recipe I'd found online, he'd seemed... distracted. His features were slightly hardened, not enough to be visibly noticeable, but enough to take note. The lines around his eyes were etched deeper, and the bags underneath were packing for a three-day trip. Even his walk seemed to be losing a spring with each step.

"Yeah, I'm fine." He sighed. "Maybe I'm just a little nervous too."

"Why?"

"Honestly?"

I nodded as a knot of insecurity balled tightly in my gut.

"Because even though I told her the truth," he hung his head, "she thinks you put me up to it, how it was all your idea, and how you want me to take the fall."

Allowing my heavy sound to punctuate the air, I pressed into the molded seat of the car. "She's never going to forgive me, is she?"

He cupped my chin and gently turned my face to look at him. "She will. Eventually. She's been angry for the better part of a decade, and she can't flip a switch and forgive quickly. Just be yourself and she'll have no choice but to fall in love with you like I did."

I sighed again, not feeling an ounce better, although Carter's words were like melted butter. "You make it sound so easy."

"It is. You'll see. Now c'mon, you need to meet Jasper. He's the opposite of Bea, and they're fun to see together."

I plastered on a brave smile. "Okay, let's do this."

We exited the car and headed up the walkway. Deep inside my pocket, my phone buzzed, and I pulled it out shielding the realtor's name from Carter's prying eyes.

"Hey, it's just Amanda. She's lost."

"Well, I can help."

"Nah." I tried to wave away the sudden uptick

in my voice. I really wanted to return this call. But I didn't want to spill the bean to Carter just yet. "Go on in, warm your sister up to the additional guests coming, and I'll join in when she gets here. She can't be that far away."

I looked at the dessert in his mittened hands.

His brows knit together, but a slow, hesitant bob greeted me. "Yeah, okay. Well, just knock and enter when everyone's here."

"Thanks." I breathed out a breathy sigh of relief.

I waited until he went into his sister's place before I hit redial. My focus jumped around, but mostly it stayed on the front of the house making sure Carter didn't come back outside and Amanda wasn't pulling up.

"Hey, Cara."

"Hugo. I'm assuming you're calling to talk to me about the offer?"

Yesterday, after viewing a few residences, I found one I'd fallen in love with. It was perfect; a two-bedroom loft with a view of the mountains, and it was tucked back off Main Street. It had everything I wanted and although the price was higher than I'd hoped, I still put an offer on it, knowing it would be tight but workable.

My heart pounded at a breakneck speed.

"I'll cut right to the chase. They rejected your offer."

With that, my heart stopped, froze, and splashed into my stomach.

"Just like that? I was flexible with possession dates, and I already have financing ready to go. Do they want more money?" I'd already offered their asking price.

"I'm sorry."

I turned my back to the house. "What about the other place? The one on Boulder? Can I put an offer on that?" My voice pitched in wild desperation. Getting away from the motel was a need, not a want.

"It's already pending from another couple."

The air rushed out of my lungs. "Can I make a higher bid?"

"No. The sellers have accepted their offer pending financing."

"I have financing."

"If it falls through, I'll be the first to let you know. In the meantime, I do have some good news."

I couldn't even venture a guess what it could be. "Hit me with it."

"I talked with the owners of Lexington about leasing the building beside Daisy & Dahlia's, and they've countered."

I swallowed. That too, had been at my maximum. "That's good news?" We apparently came from different worlds. "And? By how much?"

"I think we have some wiggle room, but they are countering with a twenty-five percent increase."

"Twenty-five?" The words spit into the cool air. Tossing the numbers around in my head, there was no way to make any of it work.

"Like I said, I think we have some wiggle room."

I shrugged and sat on the cold, concrete step; the chill seeping right through my pants and settling deep into my bones. "I can't. You and I both know the offer I presented was my upper limit."

"I'll see what I can do. Sorry, I don't have better news."

"Well, thanks for trying." I hung up and tipped my head down, fighting the tears.

Just like that, my new plans for moving here permanently and setting up a hardware store went up in smoke. Living in the shabby motel wasn't what I wanted, and rentals were non-existent. Even the housing market was quiet, which was why I'd been counting on the offer to be an easy sale, especially since I'd offered them exactly what they wanted. How could they have turned it down?

It super sucked being back to the drawing board, and now I had to go and deal with a cranky big sister who blamed me for breaking her brother's heart. What a disaster.

Where was Amanda?

Slowly pushing myself to a stand and dusting off my butt, I turned back toward the house as a curtain dropped back into place. Who'd been spying?

Headlights brightened the street and an unfamiliar car – Silas's perhaps? – pulled in behind mine.

"Hey." She exited and walked over to me. "Everything okay?"

"Not looking forward to this." I eyed the house. "She hates me and blames me for our breakup."

"Why?"

"A very long story."

With a quick glance over Amanda's shoulder, Silas joined us; a paper bag in his hands.

I shook away the sad vibes and tipped my head from shoulder to shoulder to ease the building tension in my neck. With a couple of deep breaths, I did as Carter had said, I knocked and entered a house ripe with the smell of baked ham. It was mouthwatering, and had I not had a sour taste in my stomach, would've enjoyed the scent more.

"Hey," Carter said, stumbling out of the living room. Guess I had my answer on who was watching me, not that I should've been surprised. He took a long solid look at my face, his focus volleying between me and my best friend. "Everything okay?"

I focused on his chin, completely avoiding his gaze. "Absolutely."

"Come on in. Hang your jackets there." An old coat rack already bustling with coats sat tucked into the corner of the foyer. "Come. Come."

Hand in hand, I left my troubles at the door and prepared for all new ones as we exited the hall and into the brightly lit kitchen. From a speaker built into the soffit above the dark wood cabinetry, instrumental music played. The island was packed with fancy bowls, serving platters, and condiments. My shabby glass pan with the sugar-free dessert looked like trailer trash in comparison.

"Glad you made it," Bea said, her voice tinged with displeasure. She set the last of the cutlery on the dark green placemats. "And you brought friends. How lovely." She tossed a raised brow at her brother.

Carter squeezed my hand and tugged me over to the short, stocky guy on the end of the island. "Everyone, I'd like you to meet Jasper."

Carter was right – he was the total opposite of Bea. Whereas Bea was dressed in fine office wear, complete with nylons and pearls, Jasper was wearing a flannel shirt and jogging pants, along with an apron reading *One of us is right, the other one is you*; clearly Bea's apron.

Jasper set down his carving knife, wiped his hands on a green tea towel, and shook my hand, followed by Amanda's and Silas's.

"Welcome to the family, Cara. I've heard so much about you. It's lovely to finally put a name to the face." He shook his head. "I mean a face to the name. Welcome you two as well. Amanda and Silas, correct?"

His voice was deep but welcoming, and somehow it wiped away a touch of the uneasiness I was feeling.

He sauntered back to the carving station and resumed slicing the ham. "Cara, I hear you're a marketing whiz and a bit of a trivia nut."

"Oh, yeah?" Curiously I glanced up at Carter, who wasn't trying to hide a smirk.

"Sorry," Carter said, leaning closer. "I maybe

mentioned the marketing part."

"I'm more concerned with the trivia part." I laughed and stole a quick glance to Bea, who was most definitely not laughing. Stiff as a board she glared in my direction.

"Do you play mostly online?" Jasper was either blind to the arrows being shot in my direction, or he simply chose to ignore them, either way, he gave me something pleasant to focus on.

"Amanda and I played at the bar on occasion. Friday night trivia." For good measure, I smiled at my friend. Many good evenings were had at Crocodile Jim's.

"Trivia, really?" Silas said to Amanda. I loved how they were still discovering new things about each other.

"Don't expect to win a *Friends* trivia night either. She'll smoke you." She was still the reigning champ but someday I hoped to take the title away from her.

He sliced another thick piece of ham. "I'd love to get something started at the bar."

"Are you a manager?"

A smug smile stretched out across his rugged face. "The owner." Because of course he was, it was the Ridge Heights thing to do. "And I'd love to chat with you about some ideas on getting a trivia night going."

I rolled my bottom lip between my teeth. "I'm not sure how I can help."

"With your marketing background, I'm sure you have some amazing ideas." Jasper added a slice of ham to the serving plate after a quick glance at Carter. "But we can always discuss that later. Tonight is about celebrating. No talk of work, right, my little Bea?"

Bea cracked a smile at Jasper's comment, and if it wasn't already so cold outside, I would've thought the underground had frozen over.

Silas handed his liquor store purchase to Carter.

"Thanks, Silas." Carter cleared his throat, pulled the cork out of the wine bottle, and filled three glasses with a rose-tinted variety, handing one to me and passing out the others.

Although I felt I didn't have much to celebrate, I was grateful to be hanging out with my boyfriend again and for seeing Bea's icy demeanour melt just a touch in my presence because of her boyfriend. He was a favourable fit for her.

"Bea, what can I help with?" I glanced at the table.

It was elegantly set for six, almost like it had

been purposely planned that way, with cloth napkins in rings atop the plates. The food seemed to be all set out, aside from the plate of sliced ham.

"Nothing at all. We finished everything up while you were outside waiting."

Carter cleared his throat again.

"What?" She whipped her head so fast in his direction, I swore her neck cracked. "I just mean there were only a few tiny things left to do, and we finished it off. It wasn't a shot."

Even though it felt like a perfectly aimed arrow.

MY THINKING MAY have been flawed, but I figured the way to soften up Bea was to A) be sweet, but not over the top with Carter, B) to get along well with Jasper, and C) to help Bea out with cleanup.

Over the course of the dinner, I tried all three. I lovingly touched Carter, which was impossibly hard to control and came much too easily. His jokes and good-natured ribbing kept the conversations going and even had Amanda snort laughing at one point. When I felt I had something to add, it was usually a piece of fun trivia or a factoid of some sort but Amanda could turn it into a *Friends* quote, something Bea enjoyed. With her there, my gratitude soared and the nasty feelings ticking my thoughts settled down.

Surprisingly, I enjoyed dinner, the conversations, and being a part of something, even if one of the people kept casting a nasty, albeit brief, glare in my direction on occasion. Thankfully, by the end of the meal, it wasn't every time she looked at me, just every third.

Amanda and Silas helped us bring the kitchen back to normal until it was no longer littered with dirty pans, stacks of plates, and multiple serving utensils, but sadly, they had to leave before the after-dinner walk and after-walk dessert.

I walked my friends to the door, where Silas helped Amanda into her coat.

"I'd love to stay, but we still have a bit of a drive and we both need to work tomorrow."

"Yeah, I understand." Although I didn't want her to leave. Not just yet.

She wrapped me in a hug, keeping her voice barely audible. "I like her, but yeah, she hates you. Call me tomorrow and we'll talk." Pulling back, she shook Bea and Jasper's hands. "Thank you so much for the lovely meal and the generous conversation. It's been a slice."

Jasper smiled and stepped back. "It was a

pleasure meeting you all. Next time you're in Ridge Heights, you be sure to stop in. Either here or at my bar, and we can discuss a trivia night."

Bea clasped her hands together. "Thank you for the wine. It was quite tasty."

"You can never go wrong with a bottle of rosé." Silas donned his jacket and put a hand on the doorknob. "Thanks again. Happy Holidays."

They both stepped outside into the cool air and shivered. I waved as they descended the steps onto the sidewalk, and made their way to the car and then closed the door.

"You have nice friends," Bea said and headed to the kitchen with Jasper right behind.

"How do you think that went?" I whispered to Carter, keeping a firm eye on the kitchen entryway.

"It went well, don't you think?"

"Yeah, I think so, but I think she still hates me. She kept giving me the stink eye."

"That's just her face." Carter gave me a friendly nudge. "She's always had RBF, you know that."

"But I'm not the only one who sees it." Clearly, Amanda had too.

With both of his hands on my shoulders, he tipped his forehead to mine. "Relax. It's fine. Want me to talk to her again?"

"Oh, no. It's fine. We'll assume it's the RBF." I rolled my eyes, knowing better.

"Carter, can you give Jasper a hand?" Like a cat, Bea had snuck up silently behind me.

The heat drained out of my face and a nasty wave of cool air blanketed me. Busted. Red-handed.

"What's he need help with?" He didn't seem to want to move which troubled me deeply.

"I don't know, something electrical in the movie room? Just leave and give us girls a minute. Please. I want to talk to Cara. Alone." There was a sternness to her voice which made the hairs on the back of my neck stand up.

Like an old habit, he kissed me on the forehead before retreating with two quick over-the-shoulder glances.

Bea led me into the kitchen and topped up her wine glass. She held the bottle for me.

"No, thank you."

A solid lump of apprehension lodged in the back of my throat, and I found it hard to breathe. However, I sensed a fight was on hand and I squared my shoulders, ready to take it on.

"You know, Bea, I'm trying to be nice, and I'm trying to show you that I love your brother with my whole heart, but I feel you are making things unbearably difficult."

"Unbearably difficult?" Her dark eyes connected with mine as she echoed and shifted back and forth on her feet. "Unbearably difficult, wow." With a huff, she stepped to the cabinets and pulled out a stack of small plates, which she sat on a serving tray, along with four dessert forks. Her voice was smooth like whiskey when she finally spoke after taking a long, lingering inhale. "I've welcomed you, and your friends, into my home, and you tell me I'm being unbearably difficult?"

Apparently, she was fixated on those two particular words and wasn't seeing the big picture. "Yeah. But you were great towards them, it was me you keep—"

The stern expression on her face made me pause.

"Listen, Cara, I'm not going to..." She sighed and the tight lines across her forehead dissolved. In five steps, she circled around the island, bridging the distance between us and pulled out a chair, offering me the one beside her. "Please sit."

With nervous trepidation, I moved my chair further back before I climbed onto it.

"Carter and I, we had an interesting talk yesterday, and he explained everything." She placed a warm hand on my arm, which surprised me. I figured she was the Ice Queen. "Cara, I'm sorry. For my behaviour tonight. Old habits die hard and sometimes my face gives away my thoughts before I have a chance to vocalize them."

"Okay." It wasn't an acceptable excuse, but I was going to go along with it for argument's sake.

"It's not, and I'm sorry. I will try harder." She gave my arm two quick taps. "I was watching you two tonight, and it's undeniable the attraction you share. He's happier than he's been in a long time, and I know you are responsible for it. It's just for many years, I've hated the very idea of you, so it's hard to undo that, but I'm trying. Can you understand that?"

"Maybe." It was the stupidest response, but it was all I had.

"Eventually, I'd like us to be friends again, but I know it will take some time. On both our parts." Her hands fell into her lap, and instinctively, mine did the same. "Can I ask what are your long-term plans? Carter said you were working until Christmas at Daisy & Dahlia's, but after that?"

"I don't know."

"How can you not know?" Just like her brother, she tipped her head to the side and sent a curious look in my direction.

My gaze fell to my clasped hands. "I just don't. The job situation isn't confirmed beyond that yet, and the housing situation…"

"Yes, I heard you were staying in a joke of a motel."

Wow, he'd shared that? "Yeah. I can pay weekly so until I find a place to stay, that's what I'm doing. But I need to find a steady job first."

"And Stanley?"

"We agreed on five weeks. Nothing is written, nor confirmed, for after the Christmas season."

"So you're essentially jobless by the new year?"

I ran my focus over her pristine cream-coloured blouse, and counted a few pearls on her necklace before my gaze settled on her face. It wasn't angry, or judgy but rather … compassionate. "Not yet. I have plans, well, ideas, but I can't get them to fruition. Truth be told, I'm feeling a little lost." And surprised that I actually said that thought out loud.

"Have you mentioned them to Carter? He has a lot of connections. We both do. I'm sure we can help."

I shook my head. "No, but thank you. Not telling him probably makes me a bad person. Things are going so well between us, and it's like we've picked right up from just before he moved to Europe. Everything feels right, and now that I know the truth about why he dumped me, it makes it easier to move forward."

"I imagine it would."

"But I know I can't keep renting a motel, but without a job, there isn't an anchor to keep me here, and I'm so scared. I don't want to fill him with false hope when I don't have much luck in locating something here." Voicing it brought forth a whole new level of fear. It was one thing to think about it, but when I said it and saw the pitiful expression on Bea's face, it gutted me.

"Basically, by the end of the month, you'll likely be jobless and homeless, am I hearing you correctly?"

I bobbed my head although I wasn't homeless per se. I could still rent the motel room weekly; it just wasn't ideal. "Yes, likely."

"And what then? You just going to dump my brother again when you move back to Red Deer?" In one sentence, her whole attitude changed. Gone was the soft-spoken, caring big sister tone to one of indignation, and if I wasn't wrong, it was tinged in hatred again.

"Hey, I didn't dump him, remember?"

"Sorry, old habits and all that. It's been a few years."

I snorted and inhaled sharply. "Dumping Carter was never my plan, as I want to be with him for as long as he'll have me. I'll commute if need be. I'll do whatever I need to do to make this work."

"So what you're saying is, it'll be a weekend romance, for when it best suits you."

It sounded so harsh, but there was a painful truth underlining it all. "It's better than nothing, right?"

"Absolutely false, Cara. If you're going to go all in, you need to be around for the nitty-gritty, not just a weekend of fun."

Ouch.

"You need a job and a place to stay *here* because he isn't moving to Red Deer. I need him here. It's easier for me to keep an eye on him and ensure he's doing okay." She put her metaphorical foot down, but I'd never expected Carter to move. He had a life, a job, a home, and his family here.

"I'm working on acquiring both full-time employment and a permanent home. You need to believe that."

"Well," she didn't sound like she did. "I can help with both. Temporarily, of course."

I swallowed. "How?"

She shifted on the stool, leaning back to cross her legs. "My basement tenant is moving out on December 31st, so I have a one-bedroom, one-bath, full kitchen basement suite available for rent, and I'm offering it to you."

I narrowed my eyes, feeling it was more of a keep your friends close, your enemies closer kind of deal, but still, there were merits. It was a place to live, and based on how meticulous her house was, the basement suite would be a well-maintained property. Bea would accept nothing less. However, she never mentioned what the cost would be.

Wait... Why had I even considered it for a microsecond? There would be more strings attached than would be acceptable by law. Slowly, because I wasn't the sharpest knife in the drawer, the pieces started to match.

"I suppose the job part of your helpful offer would be working at the Coffee Loft?"

A smug, twisted smile curled her lips. "Precisely. Nina can show you how to brew the perfect latte and can even teach you how to make the fancy designs on top. We pay above minimum wage and have great perks for our employees."

"No, thank you." There was zero hesitation in my words.

"You're not even going to think about it?" She leaned back in shock.

"I'm sorry, but I'm not going to work with you and Carter. Mixing business and pleasure is a horrible idea. Horrible. And living here? As lovely as the offer is, I feel you would be just too involved in every aspect. There'd be no separation. No distance. So no thank you." Working personal relationships never ended well, and I'd watched those explode in the past.

Naturally, as my voice was starting to peak, Carter chose that moment to waltz into the kitchen. He froze as he stared at me. "Am I interrupting, or are you two finished?"

"Oh, I'm pretty sure we're finished, right?" I hopped off my stool as I stared at Bea.

"We're not, but we'll end this for now."

Carter glanced between me and his sister. "You're sure?"

"Without a doubt." I faced Bea, curious if Carter knew about her proposition and if that had been the original reason she'd invited me over for supper. Going for broke, I double-downed on my words. "Thank you for the offer of renting out your basement suite and for offering me a job at the Coffee Loft, but I am turning it down."

"She what? You what?" Clearly, Carter had no idea. "Bea, we talked about this." He rammed his hands through his hair. His mouth opened and closed, and I wasn't sure if he was going to yell or bite his tongue. "I told you no, how it was a bad idea."

She walked over to him and dropped her voice to a soothing tone as she stroked his cheek.

"It's the best way. If she moves into the basement, I'll see you more because you'll be where she is. Wouldn't it be fun, all the movie and game nights we can have? We could even try our hand at a trivia night."

With a solid grip, he removed her hand. "You mean, it would be easier for you to watch over me like I was a child and not a full-grown adult. You already do that at work."

"Carter." But there was no denial or rebuttal.

The smoke billowed from his ears, and his jaw clenched tight.

The tension was thick and before more shots were fired, I grabbed him by the hand. "How about that walk before we have some cake?"

"Great idea." With his jacket barely zipped up, he stormed out of the house.

Throwing my coat on and stuffing my hands into my mittens, I joined him as he paced on the sidewalk.

"I am so sorry about my sister. That was uncalled for." He huffed out thick white clouds of steam. "I begged her not to say anything, but she did it anyway. She offered you a position at the Coffee Loft too, didn't she?"

"Yes, but it doesn't matter."

"Of course, it does. You're upset. I'm upset." He spun me around.

When I looked deep into his eyes, I couldn't lie. "Yes, I'm upset, but it isn't with Bea, and my anger shouldn't be directed at her; I'm mad at myself."

"Why? She deserves it too."

"Nah. I'm upset because she vocalized what I was thinking and hearing it out loud only made things worse." I wanted to hug him and feel his arms wrap around me, but before I knew it would happen, I needed to get the words out. "I'm upset because I'm trying to make something of myself, and I keep falling on my face."

I paced away from him, heading toward the park at the end of the block just a few houses away.

After reaching for my hand, he kept up with me step for step. "Why do you think you're failing? All I see is someone who made a huge leap in faith by packing up and moving here, who secured a job—"

"Which I only have for another couple of weeks."

"Have you talked to Stanley about an extension, or about what happens afterward?"

I hung my head in shame and watched a lady with a dog cross the street ahead of us.

"No."

"So how is he to know you want to stay? We're guys, Cara, not mind readers, and we don't take too well to subtleties. You kind of need to be more direct."

"I know. But for once, I wanted it to be…" Easy. Something I didn't have to fight for. But I didn't dare breathe that into life. Anything worth doing, I knew was worth a full effort, and having it handed to me on a silver platter wasn't what I wanted either. My dad would likely roll over in his grave if he thought for a millisecond I wanted an easier path. Probably a huge reason why I turned Bea down. I wanted – and needed – to do this on my own, and I knew that. Still…

We strolled further down the street, coming

upon an edge of a field with a lone bench overlooking a frozen lake. I took a seat, allowing the coolness to seep through my pants and settle into my bones.

"Here's the thing."

Carter's shoulders slumped, and he fell onto the seat beside me. "You're breaking up with me?"

"Oh, gosh, no. Why would you think that?"

"Just a feeling I can't shake." He pinched the bridge of his nose and closed his eyes. "I saw you on the phone, and it wasn't Amanda you were talking to. You slumped to the ground. The ground is cold, Cara, much colder than this bench, and I know you don't like the cold. So you were talking to someone else."

"Yeah, I was, and it circles back to the reason why I think I'm failing at this thing called life." I searched his face, staring into his eyes ringed in sadness. "But I'm not breaking up with you. That's not even a thought that's crossed my mind."

"Really?"

"Really."

His shoulders relaxed. "Whew, because I'm not going anywhere."

"Good." Knowing that made my heart happy and light.

"So what's weighing you down?"

I reached for his hand, needing to pull some strength from him. "I was talking with a realtor." If a spotlight was shining on his face, it couldn't have gotten any brighter. "Don't get too excited. My offers were rejected."

"Offers? As in more than one?"

A car drove by; the noise from the revving engine killing any snowy silence.

"Yeah. One for a loft and one for leasing out the building beside Stanley."

"Double—" Any and all expressions slid off his face like snow off a roof.

My voice pitched. "Carter?"

In a heartbeat, he went stiff as a board.

"No. No. No. Not here. Carter. Carter." I yelled as he started twitching.

I didn't want him to hurt himself by falling off the bench and accidentally smacking his head, or worse, shaking himself toward the edge of the embankment, so as he shook in my arms, I pulled him to the ground. Once there, teary-eyed, I grabbed my phone and called for EMS.

Chapter Eighteen

THE DOORS TO the ambulance slammed with a heartbreaking thud with an EMT and my boyfriend on the inside.

"We'll meet you at the hospital," another EMT said while walking to the driver's door.

Bea and Jasper had joined me. They'd rushed to the window when they heard the sirens and sprinted down the street to the park when Carter didn't respond to his phone.

"Let's get going." Bea was already at the corner. She didn't have a jacket on and shivered violently.

I just stood there – frozen – watching as the flashing lights rounded the corner. Without warning, tears built and exploded down my cheeks, freezing into mini waterfalls near my chin.

Flashbacks and memories to a time a few years back. It was Dad all over again, and I wasn't ready for the emotions pouring out of me. That was his last trip; the last time I saw him alive.

Everything around me was muted. Voices were foggy. Images were blurry. Even the cold didn't seem that harsh.

"Let's.... We're … good here." Her words were broken and senseless, and I watched her cross the street in a rough jog, but as I stared, it was like watching her in slow motion.

Jasper started after Bea, and once he was halfway across the street, he turned. "Come on, Cara."

Still anchored to my spot, I couldn't move. Breathing hurt. My heart hammered too hard, thunderously threatening to break all my ribs.

"Oh… for … loud." Her voice stabbed punctuated the cold air but her mouth didn't line up with the scrambled words I heard.

Jasper's strong arm wrapped around my shoulder, and he shook me gently. "The first one is always the hardest. I know it was for me."

With that, I blinkingly looked up at his sympathetic face. There was zero judgement behind his eyes.

"He's fine. Come. You'll see." He encouraged and tugged me back toward the house.

Breathless, Bea stopped at the corner. "He's going to be alright." She crossed the street and met Jasper and me halfway, unexpectedly wrapping me in a hug. "You did the right thing, and he's going to be just fine. Now, c'mon. It'll be good for him to see you when he comes out of the fog."

CLOAKED IN A haze, like a zombie strung out on too much caffeine, I followed them into the ER until I was abruptly stopped by the charge nurse and a pungent aroma of antiseptic.

"Family only." Her tone was as strict as her hairstyle – not a single strand dared to escape the tight bun, and nary a hint of warmth emanated from her tight expression.

Jasper nodded and stepped back. I took two steps back to stand by his side.

Unconcerned, Bea moved closer. "What curtain?"

"6B."

With that, Bea marched through a small group of white coats and pastel-hued outfits, heading to the back as if this wasn't her first visit.

"Go follow her," Jasper said, encouraging me toward the desk. "The nurse can take you back."

Flinching but avoiding eye contact, I clasped my trembling hands together. My voice was just as shaky. "I'm not family. I'm just the girlfriend."

"Just the girlfriend?" He tsked. "You're important to him."

I twisted my wrists and rocked on my feet. "As are you. You should be back there too."

"Nah. I know my place, and my place is the chair warmer and coffee fetcher. You're seriously not going?" He tipped his head toward the desk.

I shook my head and glanced down the endless corridor. Misery, pain, and suffering lined the hallways, and I had no desire to sneak by it. Nothing good happened behind those curtains, and remembering all the awfulness my dad went through made my stomach churn.

"I'll wait with you if that's okay. There's a lot of…" I tugged my mitts off and shoved them into my pockets, scanning the emergency waiting room as I swallowed down a sizeable taste of fear. "Bad memories."

Holding my elbow, he escorted me over to a bank of plastic chairs. We were the only visitors. Or people in the small space.

"Want to talk about it?"

"Not really."

"Fair enough." Jasper sat down and stretched out his legs, one boot loudly clomping over the other. "However," he said with an exasperated huff, "we're going to be here for a while. It would give us a way to pass the time."

I sat beside him, the chair creaking as it slid on the floor, and crossed my legs while I opened my phone and scrolled. Turning a photo toward him, my voice cracked. "That's my dad."

"Ah. You look like him. Same eyes."

I twisted to look at the last photo of the two of us together; back before things got really nasty. Absentmindedly, I ran my finger over his face as a tear slipped out.

"Did it happen here?"

Running a hand over my ponytail, I smoothed it out wishing it calmed my heartbeat too. "I'm not from here. But it happened back in Red Deer."

"I'm sorry for your loss." Like I imagined a big brother would do, he wrapped his arm around my shoulders and pulled me close.

Tears streamed again and my breath hitched in the back of my throat. "I don't mean to cry.

Especially to you. I mean, we don't know each other well enough."

"Hey, hey, hey. You had dinner at my house with my lovely bride-to-be, and my amazing brother-in-law-to-be, so I think that alone elevates you to friend status, so we're good there, plus, part of my bartender training includes a course on empathetic listening." There was a small, friendly smile accompanying his words, one I didn't have the heart to return. "Are you scared about what happened to Carter?"

The nod came fast and quick. Was he hooked up to machines? Were they filling his bloodstream with drugs to sedate him and take away his pain? Morphine had been the doctor's drug of choice for Dad, and no matter how much I told them he was still hurting, they never believed me and switched to something stronger or better.

"Cara?"

"Yeah."

"Which part are you worried about?" Without unlocking his feet, he twisted in his seat and faced me head on.

I didn't want to even say the word. Those five letters smashed together into one horrible word were the scariest ones to speak; it was torture just hearing them in my head. However, the steady stream of tears spoke on my behalf.

"You know what I think you need?"

Shaking my head, I shrugged. I didn't have a clue what I needed or even what I wanted, aside from Carter. Huddled into my jacket, I knew I was warm, and yet, I was shaking uncontrollably. A sour feeling gnawed in my gut as if I hadn't eaten in days, yet, I'd had a buffet of a meal not two hours ago. Fear ran rampant through my veins and yet in Jasper's presence, it wasn't as intense.

"Coffee. You need a cup of coffee. Unfortunately, you can't get a decent cup in the hospital, so I'm going to walk across the street…" He twisted in his seat and pointed out the window. "There's a corner store that makes an acceptable French vanilla. I'm going to grab one, and I'll be back with one for you, okay? And we'll talk. Or sit and stare at nothing. But I want you to breathe and just focus on that. One thing at a time, okay?"

Inhaling, I nodded.

"Things are easier to talk or to just be when you have a warm drink in your hands. It helps with anxiety when you have something to taste, smell, feel, and see. You just stay right here, okay?"

He rose and walked over to the nurse at the

desk before giving me a quick five fingers and a wave.

"Don't leave me," I whispered to no one.

Jasper disappeared into the corridor leading to the outside world. Through the snow, he sauntered through the parking lot until I lost sight of him.

"Don't go."

I was all alone and suddenly transported back in time to when Dad had his final trip to the hospital.

Rushed into the hospital, after I called 911 when he struggled to breathe, they forced me to wait, pointing to the brightly lit room filled with plastic and metal chairs, most filled with patients moaning and groaning. The TV hanging in the corner played *Just For Laughs* on mute although no one was laughing at the pranks. No one was watching either.

Beside the vending machine with overpriced snacks and juice, on the pitiful excuse for a side table, were stacks of ripped, outdated, but well-read fashion magazines. But it was the sounds and smells that really stuck.

Low painful moans, stifled sobs, and deep groans filled the tiny thirty-by-fifteen tiles waiting room.

Vomit reeked from the guy hunched over a

garbage can. The copper-scented blood soaked a gauze pad on the forehead of a construction worker breezed with the AC. As did the strong scent of urine, but I refused to see who that belonged to.

Rather, I tucked my stares away, waiting and listening for my name to be called with an update.

There was no clock in the waiting room. Nothing to gauge the length of time. There wasn't even a window.

Meanwhile, nurses walked around; iPads full of information they wouldn't share with me. Doctors paraded by in their runners scuffing the floor with a terrible squeak, ignoring me as if seeing someone perched on the edge of darkness wrapped in heartbreaking sobs was nothing new. I was so desperately alone. And terrified.

But that was then, this was now. Although everything had changed, it still felt the same.

Onto shaking legs, I pushed to a stand and stared. I needed to escape.

My breath laboured unbelievably hard causing spots to appear on the edges of my vision. Sweat built across my forehead and using the back of my hand, I wiped it away, smearing the dampness on my jacket.

Heartbeats pushed me past the chairs, ignoring

the silent TV, all the while fighting to breathe and to focus as I inched toward the empty nurses' station. Gripping the counter until my knuckles turned white, I attempted to read the board full of swimming letters and swirling words.

"Help me." My childlike voice called out softer than the thundering rush of my violently beating heart.

No one came. Not a nurse. Not a doctor. Not even an orderly.

My vision darkened. Memories flooded across in a sick mix of slow motion and high speed.

Four letters in bright red gave me a sign. E – X – I – T.

And just like that, I put one foot in front of the other, moving through the corridor until the outside air pulled me in. I inhaled shallow breaths as the tunnel vision narrowed to a pinpoint of light.

My words garbled, my heart stopped, and my world went black.

Chapter Nineteen

I WAS HOT; such a contrast to the biting cold. It was a comforting type of heat though, and I snuggled into it. However, something wasn't right.

Slowly, I peeled my eyelids apart and blinked in the muted light, trying to remember where I was. A heart rate monitor picked up its audible pulse. I pulled my arm back and a soft grunt filled the air.

"Hey, Sleeping Beauty." It was Carter's gruff voice.

I was lying beside him, my arm draped across his chest in some kind of death hold. As I moved, a rushing sensation flowed to my fingertips, replaced by a pins and needles feeling a few seconds later.

"We were wondering when you were going to wake up." Bea's unmistakable voice came from behind me.

"We're in the hospital?" After a hard blink, I stared at my shirt. Long gone was the sweater I wore to dinner, replaced by a matching blue snowflake pattern gown Carter was also wearing.

What happened? Why was I a patient too?

Beeps from a heart rate machine and low voices wrapped around the salmon-coloured curtain, beyond which, a patient snored. We were still in the ER.

"Why am I in bed with you?"

From under my cheek on his chest, I felt the rumble of his gentle laugh. "Because Jasper was right."

"I'm so confused." Trying to get my bearings straight, I blinked again and shook my head.

"You're confused?" Carter chuckled. "Tell me about it. I woke up here when the last thing I remember is talking with you on the park bench about rejection, but it couldn't have been me doing the rejection."

"It wasn't." I went to move but a variety of leads coming off *my* chest froze me into place. I peeked under my gown. Four were attached to my chest and one to my finger.

Bea, who I didn't even know was there, cleared

her throat and stood behind me. "I have your sweater and bra in a bag."

"What's going on?"

"What do you remember?" Long gone was her intense tone, instead replaced with a soft and comforting voice. One I'd like to keep hearing.

"Not much." Suddenly uncomfortable, I sat up on the edge of the bed. "I, we, followed you to the hospital. You went in, you followed." I pointed to Bea. "Jasper and I went to the waiting room and then he went for coffee." I tipped my head from side to side to try and remove a painful kink. "After that, my memory is fuzzy. I remember being cold, and then somehow, I was comforted. After that, there was a rush of noise and too many voices but I don't remember the details." I glanced at Bea who clearly had all the answers. "What happened?"

"Jasper went to get coffees like you said, and when he came back you had collapsed outside against the ambulance bay." She hung her head. "He saw you drop."

I gasped, and a huge dumping of embarrassment followed.

Bea patted me on the leg. "The doctors said you were having a full-blown panic attack and gave you a sedative and were ready to wheel you into another part of the hospital. Jasper suggested since they were low on beds, and if things were all good with Carter, could they put you together and monitor you that way?"

I glanced up at Carter's face. He shrugged but there was a hint of a smile tugging on the corners. Wish my smile felt like showing up, all I had was deep-seated embarrassment.

"Not surprising to us, it did the trick and you settled down." She shifted on her feet. "And you mumbled a lot."

Heat seared across my cheeks, washing over my forehead and down over my chest. "What did I say?"

"It wasn't coherent." Although the look on her face said otherwise.

"Well, thank you for staying and watching over me. I'm so sorry this situation became about me when it shouldn't have." I twisted and stared into Carter's eyes. They were brighter and his colour was good. No tubes were running out of him, no heart rate monitor on either. That had to be a good sign he was going to be okay, right?

The worry caused my heart rate monitor to pick up. "You're going to be okay, right? By the way, what time is it? How long have you been in here?"

Bea cleared her throat and moved to the other side of the bed, readjusting the curtain as she bumped into it. "It's just after midnight, and the doctors said he'll be fine. It was a longer episode than he had previously, so it's okay you called for an EMT although you won't always need to – you'll learn – but he's okay. Allegedly they're discharging him in a couple of hours. And assuming you can settle down," she tossed a quick glance to the monitor, "you'll be able to leave with him." The lines across her forehead tightened as she faced her brother. "However, he's to meet with his neurologist as soon as possible to work on readjusting his meds."

"I just need to perfect the right blend." Carter sighed and closed his eyes. "I'm almost there."

"Until that happens Carter Gabriel Cross." He winced when she middle-named him. "You need to adjust your medications. No ands, ifs, or buts. You're too important to me." Her voice took on the big sisterly one I was used to hearing, and it filled me with a sense of relief. At least some things hadn't changed. "Deal?"

He cracked an eye and stared at her. There wasn't a leg to stand on and we all knew it. "Deal."

"Okay. Good. I'm glad we finally agree on

something." Her gaze flipped between him and me as she smoothed down the front of her wrinkled blouse. "I'm going to go update Jasper, and I'll be back shortly." After she kissed Carter on the forehead, she walked back around the bed and patted me on the shoulder. "I'm glad you're going to be okay too."

With a firm yank, the curtain closed behind her.

"Sheesh, if I'd known all it would've taken for her to show you a little whatever-the-heck-that-was was to have had an episode, I would've done that a while back." He chuckled through his whisper.

"I truly hope you're kidding because that was…" Flickers of terror seized my insides.

"I am kidding, but I'm glad she showed a touch of her soft side. It doesn't happen very often." He stretched and grimaced. "Appreciate it when you see it."

"You're okay though?" I held his warm hand, entwining my fingers between his.

"I will be. It always takes a bit to fully recover." He shuffled back over on the bed, patting the space beside him. "Want to tell me what's going on? Why the panic attack?"

"The sugar-coated version or the right-between-the-eyes version?"

He cocked an eyebrow. "Hit me hard. I'm in a place where they can patch me together if I fall apart."

Even though it was meant to be funny, hearing those words, combined with what had to be a lousy nap, sent the tears racing.

"Hey, hey, hey. What's going on?"

I swallowed, not daring to sit beside him. "I was going to leave. I wanted a sign and the exit one lit up in red."

"You were going to leave?" I didn't need to see him to know his jaw hit the floor.

I stared at the floor, following a pattern until it disappeared under a chair. "Not my finest moment, I know. You called it, and I failed. The whole situation brought back too many memories of Dad, and being back in the hospital just reinforced the heartache." A painful lump nestled into the back of my throat, and I picked at a hangnail, giving it a solid yank, and then watched the blood form a nice-sized drop. "That being said, I couldn't do it, Carter. I couldn't leave. You are everything I need, and everything I want." I faced him, expecting to see disappointment and hurt, instead he was smiling sympathetically. Still holding his hand, I squeezed harder. "Somehow, someway, I'll find a way to stay in Ridge Heights and make this my home. If you still want me after my confession and knowing how hard I take things." I inhaled sharply and reached for a tissue to press against my bleeding finger. "I'm not perfect, and I scare easily; way too easily it seems, but you're all I want, and I will work hard on facing my fears as long as you're by my side."

He sat up and cupped my chin, swiping a thumb across my cheek. "Cara Louise Gallagher, I've always wanted you, and I've needed you more than I've ever let on. Your passion for things, me included," a smugness filled his face, "is one of the many things I love about you. Plus, I know you need me as much as I need you. Once you were laying beside me, you truly did settle right down."

"Do you know what I said?"

"Yeah. And I love you too."

Shaking my head, I couldn't help a weak smile. "I wish I could remember telling you; it's kind of a big deal." My heart pounded, and a wicked flurry of butterflies took flight.

"Maybe, but I already knew that."

"So… I can stay?" Hope was a flower blooming at high speed. "In my shabby motel room, working whatever job I can find since I wasn't able to secure a lease on the place beside Stanley's."

"You weren't what?"

"Yeah. That's what I was trying to tell you, before you know – the incidents. That's the phone call I got before dinner. Amanda wasn't lost, I lied." Once again, my focus fell away. "I tried to secure a lease, but they want too much money, and I put an offer on a house, but they rejected it."

"That was some bad news to get all at once."

"Story of my life." I laughed lightly. It never rained, it poured.

"You know, I was never a fan of that rundown motel room."

"I know."

"And I'd hate to see you pay too much for a rental, assuming you could find one."

"They are pricey." There were two, and each was asking more for rent than my place in Red Deer.

"Well… we'll just keep looking. And fast. I'm sure we'll be able to find you the perfect place to live. We can start as soon as we get released."

"That could be the middle of the night. I know realtors work all kinds of hours, but I'm sure not they'd be super receptive to a 3 am phone call."

He mock-sighed. "Fine. We can wait until after breakfast, but I'm not waiting until much past eight."

"You're really going all in on this aren't you?"

"Of course, with you, I'm all in."

"As I am with you. I'm sorry for my momentary lack of confidence, but it's over. It's gone. Thrown out like day-old garbage."

"Ah, Cara Gallagher, I love you. I'm sorry I had to break your heart a long time ago."

"I'm sorry too."

"And?" His whole body moved with the laugh. "You can say it now so you'll remember."

I leaned in and brushed my lips across his. "I love you too. I always have. Being fired and dumped within minutes had the best outcome."

"And we'll make up for lost time. I promise. In the past with our relationship, you're the first step-taker, and you always have been. But not anymore. I promise we'll navigate the unchartered waters together."

"No more secrets." I squeezed him hard.

"Zero."

I placed my hand on his chest and allowed a deep sigh to fill up my lungs. As I exhaled, my heartbeat slowed. "And with that, as much as it rubs me slightly the wrong way, I think I'll take up your sister's offer to move into the basement suite. It'll be better than the motel, and maybe it'll help mend the relationship. But I'm not taking a job at the Coffee Loft, sorry. I have plans to open a hardware store, and if it's not beside Stanley's, I'll find another."

"Together, we can move mountains."

I kissed him again, pulled back, and winked. "Let's just start by moving my stuff to Ridge Heights."

"As you wish. I love you."

"I love you too. Never stop telling me that."

Epilogue

Valentine's Day

"HAPPY VALENTINE'S DAY." Carter greeted me with a deep soul-awaking kiss. It never got old. "It's a big day today. Are you nervous?"

"Not in the least. I've been looking forward to this since I signed the papers."

A Christmas wish had been granted. Hugo, my realtor, had called two days after our ER visit, with a counter to Lexington. With me moving into Bea's basement suite, which she promised came with no strings, just a weekly Saturday night offer to have popcorn with her and Jasper (which I gladly accepted), it freed up more money. The new counteroffer was accepted by Lexington, and I bought them out with Dad's inheritance, becoming the building owner. It also meant Stanley was going to have to pay me rent which I wasn't a fan of, but I had plans for us both. Stanley was totally on board with all collaborations and was thrilled I was going to set up a hardware shop right beside him. I even promised him we'd do a weekly Grinch Tree night starting mid-November in my shop. It was great to be able to make future plans, and even better, to feel secure in them.

Today was the grand ribbon-cutting of Gallagher's Hardware, and hanging behind the counter was the old photo of Dad and me. The plan was to add a new photo – this one of Carter and I standing in front of the store with the ceremonial ribbon cutting scissors, along with Stanley, Bea and Jasper, and Amanda and Silas as well. The new photo will hang beside the original and I couldn't wait to have all my favourite people together, and hopefully the picture is as genuine as the one Dad and I had.

However, before the grand opening, Carter had a new drink he wanted to unveil at the Coffee Loft.

"Are you nervous?" I asked him as I wiggled on the chair, readjusting my pink sweater. Being Valentine's Day I felt pink was a necessary wardrobe choice, although not a colour I'd normally wear.

Carter agreed, and although he had nothing pink, he was decked out in a red button-up with his Coffee Loft brown apron. It suited him, and I liked the fact when his sleeves were rolled up, it exposed his naked forearm.

"Actually, I'm nervously excited. I've never made a drink like this before, but the reaction has been positive. Very positive."

"Colour me intrigued."

Everyone – Stanley, Bea, Jasper, Silas, and Amanda were gathered in the Coffee Loft, which was closed to all but invited family and friends.

The mood was lively and full of chatter, and Nina and Harry were busy holding trays full of whatever the newest drink was. Until the name was revealed, we weren't even allowed to sample.

Carter pulled down the old menu sign, the one written in chalk, and set it on the counter. Bea handed him the new sign and he flipped it over, securing it on the hook.

I read through the list of coffee names, and nothing seemed new. Until I got to the bottom one – which was closest to the eye level making it easy for the customers to see.

La Vida Mocha. It was written in a dark pink chalk.

"What is that?" I inquired with a raised brow.

"Only the best coffee to have ever come out of the Coffee Loft. It's our new specialty drink." He stepped down off the ladder, nodding to Nina and Harry.

They started walking around handing out mugs of their featured coffee.

He grabbed one from them and stood behind me, gently covering my eyes with his hand.

In a low voice, he whispered, "One shot of an exclusive espresso flavour, made from my specially roasted beans…"

He paused and my heart skittered.

"Well, you'll have to see it to believe it. It's perfection."

The scent was as intoxicating as his voice was soothing while he ran it under my nose.

"Open your eyes."

Holy beans! Before me was a beautifully layered drink in a glass mug. The three layers were gorgeous to look at; a dark espresso layer, a thick, foamy cream layer, and sitting above that was a mocha-coloured layer with a dollop of beige whipping cream. Sprinkled across the top was a brown powder, cinnamon perhaps?

"I named it after you."

"After me?"

"Well, after us. You and I, we've had a crazy life – *a vida locha* – if you will. This is our life. The dark past." He tapped the espresso layer before running his finger across the middle layer. "The missing years, where there was no flavour, just like the cream. There's froth and a bit of cohesion, but if left alone, it disintegrates. Then there's this layer, the sweet and savoury mocha layer with a little bit of kick. This represents the new us. The kick being what you did to jump-start our relationship, and all the sweet and savoury moments we've experienced since then."

Oh. My. Goodness. My heart was melting with each pounding beat. "And the dollop on top?"

"Because the best is yet to come."

"Oh, Carter." I wanted to cry, but there were people around us, staring wide-eyed at the exchange.

In slow motion, he moved from behind my right side, to stand on my left. Without warning, he dropped to his knee and pulled out a diamond solitaire on a white-gold band, lifting it high for me to see.

"Cara, will you mocha me happy by being my wife?"

"Yes!" I jumped off my chair and into his arms, loving the way he made a coffee pun into a marriage proposal. "Yes! I have *bean* in love with you forever. Yes!"

Wrapped tightly in his arms, he rose to his feet and set me back on mine. "I love you, Cara."

"I love you more, Carter."

A smug smile spilled across his face. "Hurry up and finish your special drink. We have a new shop in town to open."

**COFFEE LOFT
SERIES**

Welcome to the Coffee Loft, a place where romance is always brewing . . .

Grab your favorite table over in the corner and be prepared to be swept off your feet. This multi-author collection features some of your favorite sweet romance authors that you already know and love as well as a few new names you'll be rushing to check out. From cold brews to cappuccinos and frothy frappes, there's something on the menu for every romantic comedy reader. Fake dates, meddling matchmakers, friends-to-lovers and so much more, each stand-alone story is the right blend of sweetness, guaranteed to warm your heart. Happily-ever-afters coming right up!

Series link ➡️

https://books.bookfunnel.com/thecoffeeloftseries

Dear Reader

This story came to me out of the blue. When I signed up for the Coffee Loft series in July 2023, I had a rough idea of what I was going to write – a second chance romance – as it's one of my favourite tropes. We were given a rough word count of 25-35K words – totally manageable given the time frame. However… Cara had a few issues to unpack, and Carter wasn't exactly forthcoming in his reasons for their original breakup. And there was no way 35K was going to work. So, I got the okay to flesh the story out properly, and here it is; nearly double the goal. What can I say? Whoops? LOL. Or lucky you?

This story was also a learning experience as I had to truly tamp down all romantic tendencies and remove all the language I drop into my stories without even realising it, as this set was targeting clean romance readers (but of course, anyone who loves a great romance will also enjoy these books). All they lack is spice (but still have all the swoon!) and language. That being said, my other books are definitely spicier (but only have one-to-two open door scenes which are more emotional than graphic) but do have a lot of language, all while tackling some harder topics in the name of love. If you don't mind those elements in your stories, I encourage you to check out my other stories.

As an author, it makes my day when a reader or blogger shares their thoughts and gives me feedback on the characters they've invested their time in. When readers fall in love with a character, it's encouraging to write more. So, if you don't mind, share with me what you liked, what you loved, or even what you hated. I'd love to hear from you via email (hmshander@gmail.com), through the contact me link on my website www.hmshander.com, or a review on your favourite retailer site. It doesn't have to be long, even just as simple as "Couldn't put it down", or "Loved the characters" or "Where can I find a real-life Coffee Loft?" works. Reviews and ratings help me gain visibility, and as I'm sure you can tell from my books, reviews are tough to come by.

Thank you so much for spending time with me. Scan the QR code and receive a free series starter – Dreamers in Cheshire Bay when you join my bi-weekly newsletter.

Yours,
H.M. Shander

Acknowledgements

MY SHANDER FAMILY (Hubs, The Teen, and Little Dude). My goodness, what would I do without your unending support? Like seriously? Thank you for giving me the time and space to dive into this story feet first, to listen my rants about how it wasn't coming together, and then how it was only for it to fall apart all over again. Thank you for being my rocks. And the breath of fresh air when I needed a break. And my loudest cheerleaders. As always, thank you for all your help in market set up, book deliveries, and bookkeeping! I know I couldn't do what I love without your support and understanding.

MY AMAZING CRITIQUE PARTNER JULIE. I am so forever grateful to you for your wisdom, your insight, and all your critiques/comments/feedback you gave me on this manuscript. Once I got the go ahead for the word count, you pulled sections that needed more fleshing out, scenes that needed better explanation, and places where I was wordier than needed. You were honest, yet kind, and I know the story is way better because of your insight. Thank you for loving the characters as much as I do, and for finding all the fun Easter Eggs within. I'm beyond happy to not only call you my amazing critique partner, but also a trusted friend.

MY COVER DESIGNER REBECCA. This cover. This series. WOW. They are breathtaking and cute and adorable. Although I had no direct say in what was created (as far as colour schemes/fonts/etc), I am thrilled you produced two characters that I could easily envision falling back in love with each other. I can't wait to work with you on future projects as you were professional, timely, and a breeze to work with.

MY EDITOR IRINA. I knew if we worked together long enough, I'd find a whole new list of things for you to clean up. Ha-hah! Since this series was to be marketed as a clean romance, we both had our work in finding all the offensive words and terms I slip into manuscripts without so much as a thought. Thank you for finding them, eliminating them, and producing much better alternatives. Thank you also for your feedback on the epilepsy and helping me with that aspect as well.

MY COFFEE LOFT LADIES. Thank you for your unending support to my unending questions. It was refreshing to work on this series, to each craft our own versions of the Coffee Loft, and to forge new friendships in the process. You are all amazing and I wish you all the success you deserve.

IF I MISSED YOU, it certainly wasn't intentional. I know I couldn't be where I am without the help of so many others. Thank you! And thank you for reading and making it all the way to the end. You all rock.

About the Author

USA TODAY BESTSELLING author H.M. Shander is a stargazing, romantic at heart who once attended Space Camp and wanted to pilot the space shuttle, not just any STS – specifically Columbia. However, the only shuttle she operates in her real world is the #momtaxi; a speedy electric car that zooms her two kids to school, work, and various sporting events. When she's not zipping around in Elektra, you can find the school librarian surrounded by classes of children as she reads the best storybooks in multiple voices.

After she's said goodnight to her kids, and kissed her husband goodnight, she moonlights as a contemporary romance novelist; the writer of sassy heroines and sweet, swoon-worthy heroes who find love in the darkest of places.

For all the latest release news, subscribe to H.M. Shander's bimonthly newsletter (link available on website). Follow her on Instagram (@HMShander), Facebook (hmshander), or please check out her website at www.hmshander.com.

Thanks for reading– all the way to the very end.